Falling Free

ILLINOIS SHORT FICTION

A list of books in the series appears at the end of this volume.

Barry Targan

Falling Free

UNIVERSITY OF ILLINOIS PRESS

Urbana and Chicago

Publication of this work was supported in part by grants from the Illinois Arts Council, a state agency.

The author gratefully acknowledges grants from the National Endowment for the Arts and the Rockefeller Foundation.

This book is printed on acid-free paper.

"Caveat Emptor," *Missouri Review* 6:3 (Summer 1983)

"Triage," *Carolina Quarterly,* Fall 1982

"Dominion," *Iowa Review* 10:2 (Spring 1979); reprinted in *Pushcart Prize VI: Best of the Small Presses,* ed. Bill Henderson (Wainscott, NY: Pushcart Press, 1981), and in *New Worlds of Literature,* ed. Jerome Beaty and J. Paul Hunter (New York: W. W. Norton, 1989)

"Old Light," *Yankee,* April 1979; reprinted in *Prize Stories: The O. Henry Awards, 1980,* ed. William Abrahams (New York: Doubleday, 1980), and in *New Fiction from New England,* ed. Deborah Navas (Yankee Books, 1986)

"The Editor of A," *Georgia Review* (Fall 1979); reprinted in *Necessary Fictions: Selected Stories from the Georgia Review,* ed. Stanley W. Lindberg (Athens: University of Georgia Press, 1986)

"Falling Free" (originally entitled "The Emperor of Ice Cream"), *Sewanee Review* 91:1 (Winter 1983)

Library of Congress Cataloging-in-Publication Data

Targan, Barry, 1932–
    Falling free / Barry Targan.
        p.   cm.—(Illinois short fiction)
    Contents: Caveat emptor—Triage—Dominion—Old light—The editor of A—Falling free.
    ISBN 0-252-01645-9 (alk. paper)
    I. Title.   II. Series.
PS3570.A59F35   1989
813'.54—dc19   88-36637
                                                        CIP

to my mother

Contents

Caveat Emptor

Joey Rogovin swung in and out of the way of the hard platoon marching like hammers on the Boardwalk. Like one more in the vast undulant sheet of searching pigeons, he would move aside for the rectangle of men and then fold back in their wake. Like the pigeons, he was a gleaner. At fifteen, he was unsure of the shape of irony, yet he responded to the fact of it: heavy armies might trample down the golden fields and destroy Empire, but along the way they also smashed it into little pieces manageable by small scavengers. What Joey Rogovin in his own lifetime could never have hoped to share in now fell easily to his hand and wit, and he battened upon his luck and opportunity, for this was war.

Not that the Boardwalk was a golden grain field; not that Atlantic City was that sort of Empire. Rather, it had suddenly become the largest military training camp in the world. By the potent magic of supreme decree, it had been changed in a few months from the Queen of Resorts to the King of Armories. From December 1941 to the following April, the grand hotels—the Haddon Hall, the Traymore, the Dennis, the Marlborough-Blenheim, the Shelburne, the Breakers, and all the rest, as well as every modest sidestreet inn and even some of the larger rooming houses—were converted into barracks. Nothing else in America was so ready made, so in place, so quickly adaptable in 1941 to such a purpose as was Atlantic City.

Partitions divided space to multiply it. The magnificent suites such as that on the fifteenth floor of the Ritz-Carlton high over the

grey-green Atlantic of the south Jersey shore, that which even
through the recent summer had sheltered variously the Ludens
of the Luden cough drop fortune; the Clothiers from Ardmore,
Pennsylvania; the entourage of the mobster Louis "Thumbs"
Mangore—that suite now housed forty common men. And now
with no splendid view. All the windows facing the sea were
blacked out, darkened against the lurking eye of maurauding enemy U-boats, steel sharks waiting out in the ship channel not more
than a dozen miles offshore.

Partitions were erected or walls were ripped out, toilet facilities
were expanded, shifted, or built. Stairwells and fire escapes were
repaired, evacuation plans made, elevator cables restrung—there
were details. But in the main nothing could have been easier than
this transfiguration. The large kitchens were ready, the crystal-
chandeliered dining rooms were turned into mess halls, the par-
quet ballrooms cleared for calisthenics when it rained. And of
course there was the perfect drill field—the wide, substantial,
flat, clean, resilient, and nearly endless Boardwalk.

All day from reveille to retreat the khaki men would drill,
marching north in the inland lane, south on the seaside. Between
each element sufficient space was left, a hundred yards or sometimes two hundred, for the troops to be wheeled about and
wheeled again, to be moved from ranks into files and back, to be
dressed right, to parade rest. Order, containment—the discipline
upon which unquestioned response in battle depended—was estab-
lished here.

"Companeeeeeee . . . halt!" the sergeant would call. "Take ten.
Smoke 'em if you got 'em. Don't leave no butts."

Then it was time for Joey Rogovin.

The men on their ten-minute break could move about, but only
within the loose shape of the unit. No one could walk back a half-
block to a Boardwalk store to buy a Coke or a hot dog or gum or
cigarettes. Even if they were on the beach side of the Boardwalk
and the company had chanced to halt across from a store, they
could not cross to the opposite side. And along much of the
Boardwalk where the men drilled, that part of the Boardwalk
which before December had been an elegant promenade of elegant

shops (Wing Fat's Oriental knickknacks in jade) and auction galleries (Lloyd's for the finest lace, Boughton's for Wedgewood and Louis Quatorze chairs), along this stretch there were no hot dog stands or sundries stores at all. So often there was not time enough, and every distance was too great for the soldiers to buy anything, obedience now opening a chasm between their old lives so recently shed and the soldiery they had become.

"Cigarettes, Cokes, gum. Candy. What do you want? What do you want? Let's hear it," Joey Rogovin would shout. He would wheel his rattling balloon-tired bike around them like a herder of cattle. Quickly then men who wanted something would give him money, and on his bike he would speed down or up the Boardwalk to the nearest store and back to buy for them. He lived on the change they left him. Coke was a nickel, two cents deposit on the bottle. From the dime they gave him he made three cents, for the bottle two more. Out of a dime he made half. A hundred percent profit. This was a great country. And sometimes they gave him a tip, a nickel extra. Except for the farm boys from the middle of America—Missouri, Oklahoma, Iowa; for Joey Rogovin, the edges of the earth. The farm boys would count it out. A nickel and a two-cent deposit. Nothing for nothing. As if they had come, warned by their parents and ministers, to be on guard against the slick World. But did they think he, Joey Rogovin, was a service provided by the United States Army? All he could get from them was the bottle deposit. In time he learned to spot them, the clean white-haired, blue-eyed counters, and not take their orders if he could avoid it. Time was money, the space in his basket was money. In time he learned more.

He was not alone. He was not the only boy with a Rollfast bike and a wire basket propped out over the front wheel. But, unlike the casual boys who once or twice worked an hour or a day or two at the game of it for the dollar they might not need, Joey Rogovin was filled with a mercantile vitality, driven by the entrepreneurial imagination of merchantmen such as those who sailed from Genoa around the Cape or that once propelled caravans to Byzantium and beyond. In him there was an intensity of trade that blurred any line between need or want, though he had plenty of both.

He and his parents lived in a tiny top-floor apartment on Seaside Place, a little half-street off Oriental Avenue between Vermont and New Hampshire. But his mother—his small, gentle, fragile mother—every morning opened the door expecting an old Latvia, nubbed hills, rolling fields, high trees. She never understood the whiteness of sand, the size of oceans, seagulls, that the world was round. War. Every morning she was surprised. And one day she would at last open the door to the sturdy green earth, to the pungency of manure at work in the land of the valley a hundred kilometers beyond Riga, and she would step through, smiling gaily forever after, her patience finally rewarded, and be gone.

His father, Koslo, wherever he had come from, whenever, knew nothing, could learn little. He worked in Fineberg's Junk Yard sorting debris, shifting mounds of paper and rags into larger mounds for the bailing machine to compress and strap. In Atlantic City there were three junk yards: Snyder's and Giordano's, each as big as a city block, and Fineberg's, as small as a garage. Fineberg got the junk left over from the junk. Koslo Rogovin tended it.

At night he and his wife would sit in their tiny kitchen, winter and summer, drinking tea and listening, to what Joey never knew. Certainly not to America.

Joey Rogovin listened to America. Some nights it would pulse through him like his own blood, surging, torrential with its promises, textures, strengths, words, complexities. Or he would lie in bed and on his radio listen to Byron Syamm, the voice of the Philadelphia Athletics, inventing baseball games between the A's and the Detroit Tigers, creating the game off the ticker tape just as if he were there in the Motor City. For a home run Syamm would whack a block of hard wood with a stick. ("It's going, *going, GONE!*") Joey had read about it in the *Philadelphia Sunday Record,* this casting of the illusion. But he did not care less because of that, for beyond the illusion was the reality, the game itself. Whether Byron Syamm saw it or not, it was there, going on, men endeavoring, straining, reaching, innings, runs, stolen bases. And maybe even the game was, maybe everything was, just a sign anyway, itself a signal for something else, something tough and solid and hard as gold.

Even by the middle of that first summer, soon after the Battle of Midway, he made the first important changes, the first critical business decisions. Why wait for orders from the soldiers? What, after all, was there for them to order? Cokes, cigarettes, candy, gum, sometimes a hot dog; ice cream and Popsicles after the weather warmed up. Always the same. What they could consume instantly. So why wait to hear what you already knew? Why waste half the drill break on the ride to the store?

Joey began to follow the troops prepared, his basket (larger now, reinforced) full of goodies. A master stroke. His business doubled, tripled. Not only could he carry more and supply it quicker, but the presence of the goods, the actuality of them, made customers of the men who might not have bothered to emerge from their weary boredom or reverie or hot and gritty chagrin. For those who could not imagine the frosty Coke, the nectarish Juicy Fruit, the ambrosial Mounds bar, for them Joey Rogovin would provide both image and substance out of the fecundity of his own abundant spirit and his cornucopial basket. He would give a little to get. Good business was a two-way street, was it not? A two-way Boardwalk?

And now there were risks. Where before he was little more than a delivery boy, buying with the money of others what they wanted, his gain limited to gratuities and two-cent bottle deposits, now he invested his money, set his own prices, Absorbed his own losses.

His biggest problem was this: warm Cokes. He had to buy cold and sell cold, which meant that he had to time everything—the buying, the bringing, the selling—to coincide with the break.

A break was never a certainty. He could know neither the exact moment when it would occur nor even if it would occur at all. Different units at different points in their training cycles had different drill patterns. At the beginning of the cycle, the troops raw and stumbling, there were long periods of drilling and fewer breaks. In the middle, after about a month, more breaks. At the end, long periods of marching and much more double time, fewer breaks but longer ones, fifteen minutes, sometimes twenty. These late units were the best for him.

And he learned to identify his customers—the hesitancy of recent civilians, the unworn heels of stiff boots, the stab of blis-

ters, the wince. He didn't have to ask. Idle talk could sink a
ship, right? Instead he could listen to the complaints. If they complained about the drilling itself, they were new. Middle units
complained about the food. By the end of the training cycle the
men were quieter, more private. Soon they would be going into
specific training. Infantry, tanks. Airplanes. From Missouri and
Oklahoma and Iowa they had now come halfway to the ship waiting to take them. For them the giddy camaraderie of dislocation
had ended. These units ate and drank and smoked more, like a last
chance, or a chance ending.

And sometimes the sergeant would scream, "Awwwwlright,
you mothers. No break. No friggin break till you drop down dead
or get it going like it should. TeeeeenHUT! Foooohaaard,
HARTCH!"

And Joey Rogovin's iced Cokes would warm, his Popsicles
would melt.

Or it would rain.

There were no guarantees, only opportunities. And vicissitudes.

By summer's end he had banked an incredible thousand dollars.
He bought his mother a pyrex pot to boil water for tea, but she
dropped and shattered it in a week; for his father, the finest pair of
leather work gloves, by then difficult items to obtain. But Joey
Rogovin was learning about more than soda pop. He was learning
about the deeper luxuries of men and about the price of services
and goods.

And finally September was in the air, equinox visible in the
shifted patterns of the sand ridged on the beaches, autumn in
the different angle of the sea wrack lined out by the receded tide.
In the early bright blue mornings the men would shiver slightly
and stamp and make a collective cloud of human breath. Sometimes a block or two away Joey would see it, the gauzy cloud
hovering like mist just above them, then steaming off in the
quickly rising sun.

His sales per unit were down, went down with the temperature.
But volume over all was up as the military base expanded and
expanded again, like an organism that only inhaled. The distances

between the drilling units was shortened to gain additional space for the crowding battalions. Fifty yards now between them. And even some of the side streets—Kentucky Avenue, Tennessee, New York—were used as drill areas as well.

Joey held his own, and his own had become more. He had mechanized. Harry's Bike Shop built him a good-sized cart mounted on a bicycle-wheeled chassis that he could haul behind him. He had the box lined with galvanized metal that his father had found and saved. There was a drain in the bottom. Now he could carry ice to keep his Cokes cold, his Popsicles firm. Let the sergeants thwart him no more! With the combined capacity of the cart and the front basket, he could supply, if not an army, then at least a thirsty and hungry platoon. With two grocery stores on Atlantic Avenue he had made deals to buy their now-limited supplies of TastyKakes at double the markup. From the soldiers he could get triple that. Was this black market? Would he at last be investigated by the newly forming Office of Price Administration?

But in the bright blue days that seemed like an endless and perfect promise of lassitude that mocked the rage of war came the first subliminal lick of northeasterly winds, the gray to come, the wash of salt scud weather that would scour the Boardwalk clear of men and their appetites. Although on clear winter days they would continue to drill as ever, they would hate their breaks, and all they would do would be to huddle and curse the blade of the North Atlantic wind slicing through them.

In early September Joey tasted the season like the other native creatures in the air and sea, and he knew better than these men what was about to end.

School was threatening him as well. Not that he disliked school; not at all. He was an apt and attentive student, and he believed in the efficacy of decimals and fractions, mixed numbers and Pythagorean lucidity, the history of his nation, the structure of flowering plants, the voyaging of Odysseus.

But Occasion had come to him specially, and it would be difficult for him to relinquish what he had made of it, what he might make of it, although none of them—the men marching on the Boardwalk, the busy people of the city, even the other students his age; yea, the world and all that it inherit—none thought life would ever be the same again. They all sensed that whatever had been suspended for the duration had been suspended for good. The concussion of enemy or Allied shells falling even now at Guadalcanal had shaken apart, would shake apart, the old fabric, tearing it beyond repair. But for Joey Rogovin this knowledge, which was new to him and not comparative, had come in a more exact, a more precisely defined shape than it had for others, than it had for most.

The exact shape of the present that seemed to define his future was $1,784. Some of it had been put into war bonds. But there was more to his knowledge even than the bank account or what he had learned that his father had never grasped: the connection between Will and Profit. He had also learned that there were rules for some and rules for others: there were always rules to human conduct, but not always the same rules at the same time or place. Who mastered that knowledge would make the future and master it. The world, just now being beaten to a pulp, would in time take whatever mold was put upon it. Joey Rogovin learned this in his way from a man who taught him—in *his* way.

"Hey you, kid," Eddie Cribbins called to him. "Come here."

The profitable day was over. Friday. Fridays were always good, the best, as if the promise of the less restrained weekend awoke in the men preparatory wants. The last refrains of retreat's trumpet died. The movement of the Boardwalk, halted along its length for the ceremony of lowering the flag, started up again, but the drilling men were gone.

"Hey kid," Eddie Cribbins called to him again. Joey had wheeled his machine nearly to the top of the ramp down from the Boardwalk when he heard Eddie, his voice raspy like a small insect buzzing.

Eddie Cribbins was a Private First Class. One stripe. More than a recruit in basic training.

"I seen you working. All summer. You got a good thing," he said.

"Yeah," Joey said. But Cribbins's words sounded to him like a warning, a feint before the spring of something more.

"You work hard. You make a buck. I can see. I got eyes."

"Yeah," Joey said. "I do OK. You don't drill? You got a stripe already?"

"I'm assigned here," he gestured vaguely. Where? Joey wondered. To this building, the Chalfonte Hotel on the Boardwalk that they stood before? To the entire base? To the city itself? Who was this guy? "I'm waiting for orders. They got me lost. I'm waiting here till I get found."

"See you around," Joey said and started off.

"Wait a minute. Hey. Wait a minute. I got something for you."

"You got something for me? You got nothing for me. What do I need? See you around."

"Advice. For you I got advice."

"Thanks," Joey said. He moved away.

"Make money," Eddie Cribbins said. "That's my advice to you. Make money."

The boy stopped.

"What am I doing? What do you call this?"

Eddie Cribbins had been resting with his back against the building; now he stood straight. Even so, he was not much taller than the boy, as lean as a stretched muscle, a runner's shank of a man, but narrow, his shoulders no wider than his hips. "I been watching you. You got a good reputation, too. You hang in. You work. Reliable. Honest. Smart kid. I got plans."

"I got to get home. They're waiting." But Eddie Cribbins went on, his eyes like ball bearings in a pinball machine only dark like marble, deepest maroon and hard. Joey could see in Eddie Cribbins's eyes his own reflection.

"You want to make money? Here is how you make money." He turned and quickly ducked behind the heavy column of the arcade and out again, and in the same motion opened the lid to Joey's wheeled carrier and put into it twenty cartons of cigarettes. "So." He stepped back to the boy. "There you go. Get thirty bucks for that at least, maybe more. Fifteen bucks for me, fifteen bucks and plus for you. Fifty/fifty. What a deal."

"What do you mean? What is this?" Joey Rogovin protested, but already he understood.

"Do I ask for anything now?" Eddie Cribbins gave as an answer. "Do I trust you? Is this trust or is this not trust?"

"What'll I do?"

"Listen kid, I don't even know your name."

"Joey. Joey Rogovin."

"I don't even know your name and I hang on you thirty bucks worth of choice tobacco. Trust. I'm telling you, if you can't trust the man you do business with, you shouldn't do business with him. Right? Is that right? You're a businessman, you should know. Right? All summer I see you. You don't give no credit, right? Cash off the top, right?" Eddie Cribbins's voice sawed at the air, making fine dust of it.

"Yeah, right."

"Sure. It's the only way with your kind of operation. And when do you know you'll see these guys again, huh? So it's cash up front."

"Yeah."

"But you and me, now this is a different operation altogether. Without trust we got nothing. With trust we got a gold mine. We got a mint. We can print money. You understand."

There was much that Joey did not understand, but he understood enough so that he knew he would be able to work out what more he needed to know. For now he knew that suddenly he had a supplier—cartons of cigarettes instead of Cokes; he knew that there was no cash outlay on his part; and he knew that now he needed a customer. So nothing had changed. Up, down, left, right, forward, backward were all the same. It depended on where you looked, where you were when you needed to know where you were. But what did not depend upon position or stance or attitude at all was this: if you sold Cokes out of your trailer, Crackerjacks if you could get them, Fleer's Double Bubble Gum (already as rare as ambergris), then you might as well sell anything else. *You sold or you did not sell.* In the insubstantial welter and flux of the human condition, there was at least this rock to stand upon.

"I understand," Joey said at last. And just at that moment he also understood that Eddie Cribbins had stolen the cigarettes, probably from where he worked.

Joey and the civilians had begun to hear about fabulous hordes of commodities ordered and requisitioned and stored by the military even as civilian goods began to disappear. Rationing was coming down—sugar, meat, gasoline, Jell-O, coffee, and more. In place of the famous brands of quality cigarettes, now instead there were such imitative shreds and remnants as Marvels and Wings. Bugler tobacco loose in cans to roll your own. New name brands for foods and other goods sprang up to mask the ersatz and the use of lesser grades of things while Heinz and Kellogg and Campbell marched off into their country's service.

Eddie Cribbins had his own access to this massive store. Now he needed someone at the other end, someone to go out into the world where he could not go himself, not with impunity. He needed Joey Rogovin. Trust is what you need to trust in.

"I understand," Joey Rogovin said and pushed off on his bike.

"Monday," Eddie Cribbins said after him. "Four o'clock."

But even before he reached Seaside Place he had sold the cigarettes. Ten cartons each of Phillip Morris to Mr. Slotkin at the Delaware Avenue Market and to Mr. Fishman at Fishman's across the street, the two sources of his TastyKakes. He left for home with money and with orders—requests—for more.

More he gave them. And others, too. There was not much that Eddie Cribbins could not provide, and frequently in amounts so brazen that Joey would have to store things in his parents' apartment, lugging up to the third floor sometimes half-cases of cigarettes, boxes of Chuckles and Mars bars and Chicklets, condoms by the gross lot, bags of razor blades, vials of perfume.

His mother said nothing, nor did his father, as if Fineberg's had followed him home, though this was not junk. But Koslo Rogovin perhaps could no longer tell the difference; or maybe instead, in the way illiterate sailors could intuit their positions at sea, he knew, in a condition beyond perception, the profound similarity of all things, the fundamental form which did not change in the passage of objects from state to altered state, from a pile in his son's bedroom to a pile in Fineberg's building. Either way, at either end of the progression, wealth was generated, born, more of it, or less: for under heaven there was a price for everything. So all there was or could be or need be of truth was *transaction*. The materials, the things in themselves, were only the grass and grain of energy exchanging shapes.

Eddie Cribbins and Joey Rogovin moved their meeting place often. Smaller goods could still be passed easily near or on the Boardwalk by dropping whatever Eddie had on him into the wheeled carrier. Larger transfers needed more cover and even extra trips. Eddie Cribbins made these arrangements with some care, selecting a small restaurant or bar, the back of a bakery, the toilets of gasoline stations, taxi stands.

And Joey's movement through the city became more noticeable. October, and then November, he peddled on against the lowering days.

Who did not know what he did each day after school and all through Saturdays? But this was a city in constant motion now, as if every day was the Fourth of July or Labor Day, the hectic, transient mood of high summer the ordinary tone of daily life. For not only had the city become a major military base; like all such places through all of such histories, it also became the center for much else and many others—whores and gamblers, thieves and derelicts, the refuse of armies. Unlike most other bases, because this was Atlantic City, where apartments or even single rooms could still be rented for a season or a day, wives could come and visit their husbands, bring the children to watch their fathers marching. Mothers came bringing bundles of food. Many others, too, were simply drawn as to any spectacle. It was, after all, a long parade, this edge by the sea that was the first line between brave America and the dark evil of the Axis powers. Whatever would happen to the sacred land of the nation would happen here first.

The impulse to come to the city was like that which had brought the bonneted and frock-coated gentlemen of Washington to observe gaily from open carriages, with baskets of food and champagne at their feet, the first battle and sunny rout of Bull Run.

And indeed there was battle. Reports of U-boat sightings were frequent. Nearly every day the swift patrol boats moored in Gardiner's Basin at the end of the island would burst spuming like unleashed hounds across the seas. Local volunteers would drone out and back over the ocean like reconnaissance bees in their own spruce and canvas Piper Cubs at their own expense. Sometimes a ship would be torpedoed at night. A few days later, in an eastern on-shore wind, the oil slick would come to stain and clog some of the Atlantic beaches. Once there were bodies.

So no one bothered about Joey Rogovin, whatever they knew or suspected. If you looked closely at him, then where did you not look, where did you stop looking? So you looked another way.

Except Officer Norman, too flat-footed to enlist, too essential to be drafted, who stopped Joey one day on Massachusetts Avenue.

"What's your name?"

"Joseph Rogovin."

"Where do you live?"

"321 Seaside Place."

"You got a vendor's license? Let's see your vendor's license. And if you got a vendor's license I'll arrest you. You ain't old enough to get a license."

"So who's selling anything?" Joey said.

"What are you talking? All summer you're selling—Cokes, hot dogs, all kinds of crap."

"I took orders. I delivered," Joey said. "And this isn't summer now."

"Don't give me no shit kid, OK?"

"OK, Lieutenant."

"Open the lid, wise guy," Officer Norman said. "Open it."

He stepped back as if in the carrier there might be, what?—poison snakes, a bomb, Nazi infiltrators? Joey opened the carrier. Nothing.

"Go on," Officer Norman ordered. "Go on, go on. Beat it."

Joey reported the incident to Eddie Cribbins.

"It's the dumb ones you got to look out for, Joey. The ones that don't know how to get something."

"What do you mean? What does he want?"

"What does he want? Whatever you got, that's what he wants. He wants some of that. He knows there's action here, but he can't figure out what to do to get his. How to get it. You got to be careful with that kind. You can't just go up and lay it on him, stick a bill in his pocket and forget it. No. He's got to wake up with it in his pocket in the morning wondering where it came from so he's still thinking he's an honest cop. But we got ways to handle dummies, Joey, we got ways. And we got to get this guy fixed up before Christmas, remember that. Christmas is going to be our big season. We make it good then. We don't need nothing messing with Christmas, right?''

The plan was simple enough, and effective. For about four days Joey stayed in Officer Norman's path, peddling back and forth across his way like a gull taking large tacking stitches across a freighter until the policeman turned finally against whatever kind of resolve he had decided upon for himself and stopped the boy. He opened the carrier lid. On the galvanized bottom of the carrier rested, out of its package, a large-faced Elgin wristwatch with the new type of expanding band. New and bright and irresistible. Norman looked at it for a long time.

"What's that?" he pointed.

"What's what?" Joey said. Eddie Cribbins had instructed him.

"That."

"What?"

"That. *That!*''

"I don't see nothing."

"What do you mean you don't see nothing. Look, *look,* goddamn it."

"Nothing," Joey said. "I don't see nothing."

"*Look!*'' Norman ordered. Pleaded.

"I don't need to look. I know what I got in my carrier. Nothing. It's empty." Then he walked off.

"Hey," Norman shouted. "Hey, where you going? Come here! *Come back here!*'' But Joey walked on, about a hundred feet away. Slowly. Long enough. When he turned around Officer Norman was gone. The lid to the carrier was closed. Only when he got home did he look inside. Empty. Just as Eddie Cribbins had said it would be. So are contracts made, pledges given, bonds and covenants insured. Joey Rogovin mounted the stairs breathing in deeply. Now truly he felt expanded and bold.

Then there was the problem with Charles "Sonny" Miller.

Sonny Miller had a candystore-newsroom on Indiana between Atlantic and Arctic Avenues, but what he really sold was policy, numbers. He booked some horses. And sometimes he sold other things, out of the way, like stolen goods.

How Eddie Cribbins found out about Sonny Miller he did not say, and even then he had, as always, left the business of arrangement and delivery and collection to Joey. Still, he knew his man.

"Forty woolen blankets. Tell him. Special stuff. White, not khaki. No insignia. Nothing. Beautiful stuff. Five bucks apiece."

"Blankets?" Joey had asked.

"Why not? Maybe it's a long war. So should civilians freeze? See what he says."

The deal was made easily enough. But instead of Joey delivering forty heavy blankets, they arranged for a pickup. Sonny Miller had a car and certainly he did not want merchandise like that, so clearly traceable, in his store, even with his expensive good will in place with the law. A hundred dollars now, a hundred dollars at delivery. But after Sonny Miller threw the last blanket into the trunk, he would pay no more. A kid was a kid. Where did he get the blankets? His mother knit them? So? The kid had no leverage. What could he do? And if by chance he was working for someone, and one day large men with thick hands showed up on Indiana Avenue with clear demands, so then he would pay. Quickly. Where was there a mistake that couldn't be mended faster than a broken head? You pushed what you could push. You bent when you couldn't bend. That was all. Charles "Sonny" Miller pushed Joey Rogovin, bent him. The door slammed. The car started.

"A hundred bucks is enough," Miller said. "Plenty. What do *you* need? And it's a hundred more than it cost you." And he drove off.

But in two days—Monday, a school day even—large men did not show up at Sonny Miller's store. Only Joey Rogovin appeared.

"You want more blankets?" Joey said.

"What blankets? What are you talking? Get out of here. Once is all I'm telling you." But Joey did not leave, so Sonny Miller came around from his glass-cased candy counter and threw him out.

Miller's phone rang. Business. When he looked up from the pad he was writing on, Joey was back in the store. Miller threw him out again. The third time he threw him out he hit him, a stinging smack across the face. The fourth time he threw him out, he kicked the bicycle until the chain broke and the front wheel twisted and its spokes pulled out. Ruined.

But Eddie Cribbins had taught him that there was a business to threat. You make a man know what you're willing to do, and once he believes that, then you're back in business again. Either he pays the price or you do. It's a tough negotiation, but at least there are limits, terms can get worked out. Sometimes it's better to write it off, take a loss as a loss and don't pretend. But if you want to deal in pressure, then make the pressure clear right away, just the same as if you were selling something else. This is this, this is that. Take it or leave it. No discounts.

So the next day Joey Rogovin was back at work. Earlier. Right in the middle of the early morning traffic when most of Miller's numbers business was going on, people hurrying to work placing their nickels and dimes or even quarters on three numbers, sometimes boxed, a deposit on a dream waiting at the end of the day, a chance on tomorrow.

Miller was too busy to throw Joey out of the store more than once, and too surrounded by his customers to do anything else, to scream or beat him. But he threw him out twice before lunch and three times after. And he hit him hard now, sometimes hurting him right down to the bone.

On the third morning, when Joey Rogovin showed up, bruised and on foot, Charles "Sonny" Miller paid up.

"Here," he said, white, defeated, a bubble of small terror even clogging his throat, "Here." He pulled the money from a bundle in his pocket and stuffed it into Joey's hand. "Now get out. Go."

"The bike," Joey said. Miller yelped as if now he had himself been battered, but he pulled another ten dollars off his roll.

"Here. That's all. That's it. Now get out. Come back again and then I'll show you something. I'll break your arm. I'll break it twice, here and here, I swear to God."

But three days later, when Joey Rogovin did return with a new bike, when he entered the store late in the afternoon, Miller slumped.

"I told you. I *told* you!" he shouted, but his voice was thin and he stayed behind the counter. Joey looked around. The store was empty.

"I got ten silver identification bracelets. Pure silver. Heavy. Eight bucks."

Miller looked at him. Was this true, that he had come back?

"You're crazy," Miller said.

"I'm in business," Joey said. "I work for a living."

"Six," Miller said. "Six bucks."

Joey shook his head. He held up a fist and two fingers.

"No. Seven is too much. No. Six-fifty. Six-fifty is as far as I go."

The boy and the man shook hands across the glass counter that housed the moldering squares of Klein's Grade A chocolate and the faded blue boxes of Jawbreakers. Then the boy took a small brown bag out of his coat pocket and gave it to the man, who went into the back room and examined the contents carefully. When he returned he measured out thirteen five-dollar bills and handed them to the boy.

For Christmas Joey bought his mother the only good coat she had ever had in her life, though she seldom left the apartment and the coat was beyond her need. That was what he wanted to give her, an idea about her possibilities here, a coat that might make her dream in America. But she did not change. Maybe she imagined that someday she would use the wonderful coat trimmed with fur in Riga, where there were winters deep and long and white. For his father he also bought clothing: workshoes with steel-protected toes, and a leather jacket to protect him from the sparks that flew at him like tracer bullets and burned holes in his shirts and scarred his chest when he cut up scrap metal with the oxyacetylene torch at Fineberg's. For himself he bought a fine radio, a Zenith with a magical green cat's eye that winked and squinted as the tuning dial spun through thousands of megacycles. On the radio, which he connected to an aerial on the roof, he could hear short wave and ships at sea dotting and dashing to destinations and to each other. Sometimes late at night, after listening to the gabble of foreign voices that increased with the darkness, he would go to the roof of 321 Seaside Place and look up at the winter-brightened stars and the white constellations they etched on the black sky and he would wonder where they all were.

In his bank book, deposited at one and a half percent interest, was $3,532.18. At sixteen, Joey Rogovin was a person not only of some financial means but of some highly fluid property; he was in possession, too, of an experience as rich and patterned as a stiff brocade, as tough and durable as sailcloth.

Joey and Eddie Cribbins met at Kornblau's Delicatessen. Eddie was drinking tea, Joey ate a large Kornblau Special: corned beef and coleslaw on rye with oozy Russian dressing. Eddie Cribbins had a bad cold, and it drew him in even tighter; he looked squashed, as in an accident. And maybe that is what had happened, an accident.

"They found me," he told Joey.

"What's that mean?"

"I was misplaced, now I'm found. I'm getting shipped out. To England." He body tightened another notch. He would squeeze into nothing and disappear, leaving this calamitous world altogether.

Quickly Joey looked around the restaurant. Who might have heard? What spies might there be even here in Kornblau's on Virginia Avenue? Maybe something of what he heard at night on his radio came out of such inadvertence. Maybe even this would be sent in code, tonight, Eddie's indiscriminate information. Joey had seen the war movies. A hint here, a word there, a slip of the tongue; soon enough the picture laid out across the plotting board of the Atlantic Ocean in Command Headquarters in Berlin would be classified, and another convoy of Liberty Ships would be in danger as the sinister admiral moved a wolf pack into position with a long stick, like a croupier in a great game.

"Hey, Eddie," Joey said. "You shouldn't talk about troop movements. You never know who's listening."

"Fuck it," Eddie Cribbins said. They were silent then. Joey continued to eat, hoping Eddie would say no more, say nothing else that might endanger others and even him.

At last Eddie said, "So that means we're out of business."

Not until then did that fully occur to the boy.

"Yeah. I guess that's so," Joey said, holding his sandwich away. "We did real good, though, Eddie. While it lasted."

"We ain't done yet. I got a good idea. A last but very big score." He pulled at his nose with a sodden handkerchief.

"Yeah?" Joey waited. Eddie sipped his tea.

"Only this time it works different. We make an investment. This time we buy. Some very very very special goods. I'll need five hundred from you. Five from you, five from me. Just like always, right? Fifty/fifty."

"Five hundred," Joey said. "That's a lot of money."

"What's the matter? You ain't got $500 left from all you made?"

"No. I go it OK. It's just a lot, that's all."

"What's the matter, you don't trust me? All of a sudden, now I'm leaving, now you don't need Eddie Cribbins, the door is closed? Is that what you mean? Shit. What a world."

"I trust you, Eddie. Just like you said when we started. I'll get you the money."

Two days later he handed Eddie Cribbins the envelope. In two more days Joey would make the pickup at the Paris Coffee Shoppe on Ohio Avenue, just by the hospital. They had used it many times before.

"What am I selling, Eddie?"

"Don't ask. Not on this one. You'll see. It's very small. We'll make a bundle. But don't ask; not now. Be surprised. You'll be surprised."

Joey was surprised. Eddie Cribbins did not show up, either at the Paris Coffee Shoppe or ever. He was gone. After a week, Joey was sure of it.

February, March, the British army entered Tunisia, the U.S. 43rd Infantry occupied the Russell Islands, and the first reports

from spring training camps as the Yankees and the Dodgers and
the Giants stretched their war-depleted limbs. And still Joey could
not easily heal, could not shake out of himself the clutter and
shards of what had broken. Not that it was simply the money; he
had plenty left of that. Besides, money was only the abstraction,
only another sign of a greater potency, like Byron Syamm, who
would soon start to swing his miniature baseball bat against his
maple block. No. There was here a violation deeper than any balm
of money could touch or heal, a sundering so profound and exquisite that philosophies were born in the contemplation of it, and po-
ets sang its history. But Joey Rogovin had no words for any of
this. All he could do was throb with ache for all lost conditions,
the fatal act that casts us all out into what we are. He would throb
and ache and shudder but have no words to describe the birth in
himself of unaccommodated man. Until, one restless night under
the dawning spring sky on the roof at Seaside Place, Joey Rogovin
thought maybe he had been wrong: maybe under heaven there was
no price for anything. Maybe there was no value to anything at all.
No strict accounting. And all was dross: the stars, the sea, the
hammered gold enamelings of men. The hearts and words of men
most of all. Maybe, after all, only his mother in her dream and his
father pushing his life along like a bundle of soiled rags could read
with any authority a truth.

The summer of 1943. The Allied juggernaut began to move like
a great charger mounted with the armored knight as in a medieval
tapestry of battle, the relentless pace increasing, the earth shaking
with each lengthening stride. That summer Joey returned to the
Boardwalk, but more elaborately. He bought five units—bikes and
carriers—and hired boys to work for him; he showed them how.
He set up his own distribution system, buying his Cokes and Popsicles directly in wholesale amounts, and whatever else he could
purchase from whoever had something to unload. There were
shortages of everything now, and much was gone; but there was
always something left to work with, however shoddy.

Sometimes when he examined the thin, brittle covering of bitter
chocolate dipped sparingly over the spongelike marshmallow sub-
stitute, he would think of the military warehouses outrageously

stuffed with Tootsie Rolls and Clark bars, the sealed and stenciled cardboard boxes of Dentyne and genuine Necco wafers. The tobacco of the millions and millions of cigarettes turning dry and dusty. Profusion. Glut. Waste. Sometimes, too, he would think of Eddie Cribbins, though not in anger. What he thought or how he thought about him he could not tell, only that his mind then seemed to grow flat, listless, as if he were looking at a picture of something rather than being alive with weight and mass and motion, as if he could rub his life between his fingers and feel nothing. He did not like the sensation, and less and less did he allow himself to think of Eddie Cribbins.

Besides, now he had much else to think about in any day or hour, not least his delicate and tenuous relationship with City Hall and its crablike minions, official and otherwise; with the Military Police; with occasional penny-ante thugs, incompetent workers, unreliable sources of supplies, price-gouging marketeers. A day's work/worth of aggravations, and a lubricious percentage of his income to calm the stormy waves of greed lapping all around him.

Now he *was* required to buy a license for his vending. He made Koslo Rogovin the head of the business, the president of Rogovin Enterprises, but only for his legal status as an adult and thus for his signature, though his father could hardly write his name. (Koslo continued on with Fineberg, another magnate.) Joey paid taxes, direct and implicit bribes, and rent on the space in the building he used to store the bikes and his merchandise. He bought a large used refrigerator for his Cokes, a little stove for hot dogs. A dollar here, five dollars there, ten and twenty to police, detectives, dangerous characters, health inspectors, and self-appointed guardians of certain streets and some choice business areas.

But Joey Rogovin took no belligerent defensive posture; he was all offense—a tactician, a Halsey, a Montgomery, a Patton of commerce. Against the complaints of the Boardwalk stores that he was illegal, that there were ordinances against vehicles such as his, that they paid property taxes and he did not, that he was hurting their businesses by unfair competition—Joey moved beyond the Maginot Line of argument (which he could lose) to the solu-

tion of the flexible strike force. He gave to magistrates their trib-
ute and tariff as if they were his partners, gave to them before
they needed to ask, as if it were their due. The merchants of the
Boardwalk went to protocol and to law; Joey Rogovin went to his
bank account. He did not want to win a position or make a cause.
He wanted to stay in business into September. He didn't want everything, or even to be right. Who could grant him that? All he
wanted was ninety days of summer. For which he was willing to
pay, and pay well.

That summer was full of sun and the fumes of victory. The Rus-
sians began to move westward, pressing the Germans back. To his
father, the corporate president, he gave a bank book with a thousand dollars entered. He put much of his now considerable money
into war bonds and considered stocks and went back to high
school. They studied Hannibal, *A Tale of Two Cities,* the theory of
valences and the balancing of equations.

In 1944 the city began to change once more. His Boardwalk
business declined, though other ventures beckoned to Joey now
that he had a car, a 1932 Chevy coupe in good condition. But now
the city began to receive back the men it had trained and sent
forth. From the world's largest basic training camp it was turning,
as quickly as before, into the world's largest convalescent hospital, for a broken man can lie as neatly in a barracks bed as can a
whole man. The largest hotel, the Haddon Hall and the connected
Chalfonte, became the Thomas England General Hospital, *me-
mento mori.* Other barracks hotels followed as the line of war
coiled across Europe and the Pacific.

Now over the worn cedar Boardwalk instead of the muffled syn-
chronous thud of marching men came the soft, susurrant whine of
wheelchairs. Instead of the broad khaki strokes of columned men,
now dabs of men dressed in different colored robes walked slowly
or hobbled on crutches or rode in wheelchairs pushed by white
nurses, sometimes blue-caped in a sea breeze, a wind from Nor-
mandy, Cherbourg, Rheims. Through the summer the names of
victories fell on the Boardwalk like drops of blood.

Some training did continue, and Joey kept two bikes at work.
But mainly the wounded could get to the stores themselves,

though they had small appetites and little thirst. Even the men still confined to the wards had attendants that prevented his business from entering there successfully. So many volunteers poured out of the city into the hospitals that they needed to be scheduled, given proper shifts, and they brought gifts of just what Joey would have to sell, every man a hero.

He gave it up. And he was sick of war.

In a year he would have to register for the draft. Even with the strong likelihood that the war would be over by then, still he would probably be pulled in for a time, part of the army of occupation that was already being discussed in the newspapers and among his more vulnerable older classmates. But what had he to do with that? For the first time in a long time he thought of Eddie Cribbins, of how Eddie Cribbins must also have felt this way, that he had no purpose in war. War belonged to others, not to merchants. Eddie Cribbins. To think of him now.

And then Joey saw him. A pretty, starched nurse wheeled him along. He had no left leg. Nothing right up to where his body began. Joey followed behind them, maybe ten yards. The jolt of his discovery, his excitement pushing him after them—he wanted to run up, but he kept his distance. Could he have been wrong? At Michigan Avenue the nurse turned the chair around: Eddie Cribbins, without a doubt. Only now in his face there were a few small holes, a rip or two, a rough closure of flesh, on his forehead two white streaks of scar tissue that would never again grow tan. His shoulders were so close together that they seemed to touch his chin. Eddie Cribbins passed not two feet away and did not recognize him. Recognized nothing. The tide of war had washed him out across the sea and now had brought him back, a piece of flotsam.

"Eddie," Joey called. "Eddie." He went after them. "Nurse. Nurse." She stopped. "This is an old friend of mine," he said. "This man is Eddie Cribbins, right? He was stationed here once, a couple of years ago. I know him. I know him good. Eddie? Eddie?" he said. He bent down to look closer.

The nurse said, "He doesn't say anything. He might not recognize you." She paused. "You understand?"

Joey stood up.

"Yeah," he said. "Sure." She started to push Eddie Cribbins away, but Joey put out his hand. "Can I visit him? Is that possible? When? Where is he?"

She told him he could visit and then rolled off down the Boardwalk. Overhead a Piper Cub floated out over the ocean in the last automatic patrolling, the blurred memory of a search for a fleet of danger now broken and sunk fathoms deep.

Even with the trilling of the excitement in him, Joey waited two days before visiting Eddie Cribbins on the eighth floor of Thomas England General Hospital. It was for him a grisly scene. None of the men on the eighth floor had all their limbs. They were housed together as if they should support and comfort each other in the sharing of mutual incapacity; or perhaps they were kept together to prevent the spread of a morbid infection of the soul.

Eddie Cribbins shared a room with seven other men. When Joey entered, he was in his wheelchair looking, staring, out the window, which had now been scraped clear of blackout paint. On the horizon little smudges of trawlers pulled at the sea.

"Hi, Eddie. It's me. Joey. Joey Rogovin. How you doing?" But what could he ask? What could he say? What could be done with words now? "It's been a long time. What? Two years, two and a half?" He waited. "You need anything? You want something?"

Behind him a man without an arm said, "He won't talk. He hasn't said a word since he got here. Two weeks. Not a word."

"Why not?" Joey asked, and looked back at Eddie Cribbins, who had not moved. He turned again to the one-armed man. "What is it? Is he deaf? He can't hear, maybe?"

"He can hear," the one-armed man said. "He can hear what we're saying right now. He does what he's told. He goes to the mess hall. He watches the movies. He can hear."

"He can hear us now? Eddie?" He turned again and put his hand on his shoulder. Joey was bigger than Eddie Cribbins now, a good deal bigger. "Eddie, is that right? Can you hear us? Can you hear me?"

"He can hear," the one-armed man said.

Others in the room were watching now, turning from gin rummy and dominoes, a jigsaw puzzle, turning from the tedium of a convalescence that would do them no good, the men without legs and arms, hands, feet.

"Eddie, goddamn it, *speak*. Say something." He flushed with a confusion and turned now to the audience. "What is it? Shell shock? Something like that?"

"Why don't you get out of here, kid," someone said.

"Yeah, kid, something like that," another man said.

"Shock. Sure enough," a long, heavy man with both legs gone said. "But not shell shock. All you do is wake up one morning and half of you is gone. After that you got nothing to say. What's there to say?"

"Will you shut up? Will you get out of here?" the other voice rose.

"Eddie?" Joey shouted at him now. "Eddie!"

"Get out of here. Get out of here," a new, dark, furious voice rose behind him. "This is enough of a crap house already. We don't need more of this. Go away! Leave the son of a bitch alone."

"Eddie, say something!"

"Get out of here! Leave him alone!"

But he could not. He had been too intimate a partner, and the old pain of lost worth had been wrenched up in him again from the Paris Coffee Shoppe, the old dissolution, the terrible crack of doom. Now let Joey Rogovin stand forth against the dull brute of such chaos. Gently he took Eddie Cribbins's head and turned it toward him. He looked into his eyes to end discrepancies, to give him mercy, but what he saw there—the milky cataracts of hopelessness—was obscene.

He took his mercy back to save them both. To save them all.

"Where's my five hundred dollars, Eddie? I want my five hundred dollars!" He shook the ragged head a little. "I'll give you a break. I'll forget two years of lost interest, OK? My contribution to the war effort. You hear. OK, so understand." He shook him again. Harder. "Five hundred dollars, Eddie. Five hundred

dollars! This is no joke. When, Eddie, when? Soon.'' He took
him by the shoulders now and shook him until the head jiggled
and lolled.

Behind him Joey heard the strain and twist of apparatus, leather
and wire, hinges, Bakelite and steel as the restive men moved to
anger, but he had business here to do, a deal to complete. Anger
was for warriors, the fuel of war, a fire that ate itself and then
went out. But debt, not ashes, made bricks; debt surveyed the
crummy deed on the land east of Eden. Joey Rogovin was not
angry. He was making the only demand that could be made
for what alone would last when names like Iwo Jima and Saipan
and Okinawa were erased and instead reinscribed by new names,
and those in time by others. Eddie Cribbins had to pay so that
once more there could be asserted the worth of letters of credit,
bills of exchange, articles of commerce, documents of commis-
sion—all the redeeming instruments of faith that London would
honor Zurich again, New York Milan, Paris Katmandu. For under
heaven there was nothing at all but what we *agreed* to.

"Five hundred dollars, Eddie. I know you. You've got it somewhere. I don't care how you get it here, but *do it*. *Get it*. Because
you know me, Eddie. I'll get it. I'll get it out of you. Pay, Eddie.
Pay up!''

They reached him even as their howl did, and they grabbed for
him. But in the country of the maimed, what could they do to the
whole man? Joey turned and knocked them down and away. His
shirt ripped. A chair wheel pinned his foot for a moment, a crutch
cracked down across his shoulders. Chairs spun off into other men,
the card tables splintered, the dominoes clattered to the floor like
hail, the jigsaw puzzle of a serene lake in Wisconsin was jolted as
if a large stone had been thrown into its center. But he beat them
down and grabbed Eddie Cribbins and shook him harder than ever
and screamed at him above the shouting, the curses and the cries,
and now the scurrying in the outer hall of the orderlies summoned
to the alarm.

No more. Let there be an end. Let there be Awe that we are
capable of Consequence, that it can guide if not succor us and
make us human, whatever else human might be.

"You made a deal, Eddie. You made a deal, you finish a deal. Five hundred dollars. When?"

Then Eddie Cribbins spoke, redeemed at last by choice.

"Fuck you," he said, faced once again with alternatives. "Fuck you," he said. And lived.

Triage

Already this day and the two that would follow felt like a memory. A period of reflection that seemed to push forward, but only in order to pull the past into a significant shape, an informing shape, the way photographs taken at family picnics will always turn out to be about the past, losing the present even in the instant when the shutter snaps, the way burning wood gives up the heat of the sun from decades ago. There is only the past.

Philip knew about memory or, more precisely, he understood the technique and tactical use of memory. He was a writer, and like any other tool in his kit, he had the obligation to possess such knowledge. Or was it merely a skill? Knowledge or skill, it was also more than either. And now, with the perfect snow still falling (but only slightly after the two days of storm), the sharp and clearing weekend before them, the old-style VW beetle kicking and scrambling up the snow-clogged mountainside road to Garnet Hill Lodge, the whooping boys in the back seat, his friend Arthur Cullen hard as a stone with his eternal concern sitting hunched beside him—now it all had already begun to feel like a memory, a tale they would sit around winter fireplaces and narrate years hence, after they had left the mountains for good.

That is what he meant about this phenomenon, the memory phenomenon. He had even appropriated some chic contemporary physics to make a metaphor to explain it: the closer you approach the speed of light, the more events actually bend around you. The faster you go forward, the more you catch *what is already behind you*. This is why the speed of light is the universal constant: nothing can move faster than the speed of light because there is no such thing as *faster* than that. It is the limit, the moment, the point where time disappears and all you can have is the idea of the *history* of the event, the residue of motion, the fumes of the ionized air through which you have passed, the ashes.

At Wiggins Hollow, where the road descended for fifty yards before turning upward in its steepest but final ascent, he stopped the car and ordered the boys out to lessen the load and to push when it might be necessary. The lodge people had plowed the road earlier in the day, but unaccountably they had not yet plowed it again for the weekenders who would be arriving. The VW took a run at the slope, leaving the boys behind, but they caught up just as the old car needed them to shove it over the fulcrum of the hill upon which their happy weekend would balance.

That morning, until noon, when the boys had come home early from school and they all had assembled and left for Garnet Hill, he had worked on his hospital piece, an article that he had written on finger-crossed speculation (though with some encouragement from his letter of inquiry to *The Atlantic*). The essay was about the contemporary hospital, how it had, in twenty-five years, become the conceptual center of medicine, incorporating all its functions: diagnosis and treatment, but education and research and even an active civil defense role, too. That last, the civil defense aspect, was what he was working on now, and it would finish the piece. Yesterday he had gone with the hospital on a triage exercise. Triage, a noun from the French *trier*, a sifting, to sift: "a system of assigning priorities of medical treatment to battlefield casualties on the basis of urgency, chance for survival, etc." He had asked Dr. Protherton what the "etc." meant.

"This is the way it works," Dr. Protherton explained. "It was worked out in Korea and extended in Vietnam, but it has the same application in a CD event, anything from an accident or an earthquake to a. . . . "

"A bomb?" Philip asked.

"A bomb, yes," the doctor went on. "Simply, you set up categories. You make a quick decision about, first, those who can be sent back for treatment because they're not so badly hurt or because they can be moved. Second, those who can *probably* be saved if you work on them right away where they are, right in the field. And third, those you do not try to save at all. Those who are firmly lost."

"*Firmly* lost?" Philip smiled at the doctor's felicitous phrasing.

"Yes."

"You do nothing?"

"Nothing to try to save them, no. You might give a shot of morphine for pain." He paused. "It sounds heartless, but the logic is this: if you try to save everyone, even those you can't, then you'll lose more in the long run."

"So you've got to cut your losses, right?"

"Right," the doctor said. He paused. "It's a lousy choice. Even if you know it's right, it's hard for a doctor to walk away, to write off a life. You always think *maybe*. But you're wrong. You lose a three that you decided to work on and you're probably losing a couple of twos that you could have saved. So you've got to walk away. You can see that, can't you?"

"Yes."

Then they had gone out into the training exercise that was using National Guardsmen as casualties. There he could see it, the theory of it, at first hand. All day he followed Dr. Protherton through the area of the mock catastrophe as he explained to groups of medical people the complexity and plan of catastrophe medicine. And about triage. A red tag got you a ride in an ambulance or a helicopter. A yellow tag got you a corpsman or even a field doctor. But the firmly lost got nothing.

Timothy, his son, wanted to ski at once, to leave the car loaded just where it stood before the lodge and to stamp into his skis and take the long, wide, loopy run down to Thirteenth Lake. He tested the air, sniffing it, finding the heft of it, the air, the snow, the ending light.

"No problem," he announced, wise as an Indian. "We'll have plenty of light and the wind won't come. *No wind.*" He wanted to make that emphatic to his father, but far more so to Arthur Cullen, the father of Max, who stood with Timothy as posed as he before action.

Arthur Cullen had his doubts; he always had his doubts, as if the pleasure he sought was found in his more dour confirmations. But he was good company, too, a happier kind of cynic, a sour wit like a puckery wine is sour, not sour from spoilage or decay. And he was the father of Max, Timothy's closest friend. They were all close friends, veterans of countless adventures from back before the boys could carry their own gear or build a fire—or decide about the conditions of anything: camping, hiking, canoe trips, fishing, skiing. The Mets and the Knicks.

"Come on come on come on," Timothy shouted and danced.

But they settled into the lodge first, arranged their rooms, ate the soup they should eat. Then they went out to ski down through the empty monochromatic woods where every object lost a dimension in the flat white world. The trees became flat as strokes of calligraphic ink and the hummocks and rises and dips of the trail were all flattened, telescoped, so there were no distances that you could gauge because there were no shadows, no curve or mass to anything. All that was left was the movement itself and the slight slurring hiss of the skis in the unpacked but light snow. And even the sound was absorbed by the laden air, absorbed as if by a sponge until even thought and nearly consciousness itself was drained out by the porcelain filter of the white world. Finally all that remained was the distillation, the essence of movement, the motion, without sound or taste or odor and with little sight. Only the pressure of gravity was left to bind you to earth, to anything at all.

At breakfast Timothy and Max plotted the strategy of the day, the attack they would make upon Garnet Hill, Thirteenth Lake, the Siamese Ponds and Puffer Pond trails. There was bellicosity to them, if no anger; their passion was in the purity of the conquest itself, so much terrain to be engorged, miles of trails to be claimed, boundaries to be pushed back, a country to be annexed.

They produced maps, a crude mimeo-type map that was provided by the lodge with the trails dotted and dashed and named

and numbered. The important landmarks were indicated—the
gravel pit, the railroad crossing, the stream inlet, the ruins of the
Old Forbisher mansion. The other map was a United States Geo-
logical Survey map, a fifteen-minute section of the Thirteenth
Lake quadrangle. This map, the serious map for adventurers, gave
an exact profile, a definition of the land in twenty-foot intervals.
This was the map that counted. It was on this map that Sawmill
Road turned into a switchbacked, thirty-degree cliffside-hugging
ledge, or where North Mine Road jerked like a spasm down from
the mountain's higher region.

The boys decided that they, the four of them, would run Sawmill and North Mine that afternoon. Their plan was direct and
fierce. After a leisurely morning down to the lake again and over
the length of the lake and around it to Cooper's Point, they would
not return to the lodge but would instead make straight across
country and up to the beginning of Juniper Road and thus, by
stages, work further up to Sawmill.

"Where it gets good," Max said.

"Good? You mean steep," his father said. "You mean fast."

"It's not so steep. Look," his son measured the closely bunched
thin brown contour lines.

"Yeah? Well, look again. It's steep as in *narrow*. Look at the
turns you have to make. This is cross-country skiing we're doing,
Maxy, not downhill, not slalom."

Timothy turned to his father. It would have to be his decision.

"That's a lot of skiing," Philip said. He knew he could never
turn them from their triangulations and measurements, their
compass headings. Their campaign. But maybe he could diminish
them a little. He studied the maps. "Look. If we cut back
here from the lake, that would save us three or maybe four miles."
He put his finger on East Cove. "If we're not coming back
to the lodge for lunch, then we should give ourselves more time
to get up here." He ran his finger over the high route. Even the
paper seemed rough and treacherous, as if the crumbs of his
breakfast toast had cast auguries of obstructions for him. But he
defied auguries. Or at least could not accept them.

"Jesus," Arthur Cullen said, insisted. "We can't do that. We'll need oxygen. We'll need support teams. Sherpas with supplies."

"We can do it," Max Cullen said. "Sure we can."

"Sure," Timothy said.

"Maybe you," Arthur said, "But I'm talking about him and me. The old folks."

"He can do it," Timothy said. "He can do it," he said, pointing his ski pole at his father.

And so it was decided. They folded their maps, assembled and adjusted their equipment. Arthur used a no-wax composition-base ski with a fishscale pattern under the foot; the others used traditional wax. It was a totally green wax day—new snow at 20 degrees with no sudden changes likely. Maybe later in the day they would use a blue wax kicker under the foot. They buckled on their knapsacks, full now with lunch and extra clothing and emergency food and extra ski tips. They snapped into their skis. The boys lowered their goggles like visors to helmets, swung their poles as lightly as pike lances, adjusted their parkas as if they were breastplates, and were suddenly gone.

"Tally ho," Philip shouted to Arthur and followed the boys on yesterday's trail down to the lake, but even by the first bend he had to haul up and wait for him.

The morning was alight. It could have been an entirely different trail from the one they had been on late the day before. The last of the storm, the low pressure trough that had brought the snow, had passed in the night; the day was high-pressure clear, too winter tight and dry for any clouds to form. The temperatures would start down even in the sun, and overnight would bottom out. Tomorrow, Sunday, would be as cold as winter got. But today, today was blazing with light and warm enough that way. Warm, too, in the exertion of the cross-country skiing itself. And warm in the exertion of friendship.

By the time he and Arthur reached the lake, the boys had skied across it to the western shore. Even now they were circling out and around on the lake in the unpatterned swirl of an energy incapable of being leashed; like unstoppered flagons, they would spill their force until it was gone with never a thought about it. They would be full again tomorrow, for they were magic vessels.

At the edge of the lake the two men sat on a boulder knocked clear of snow. They broke into their first candy bar and waited for the boys to come back.

"Were we ever like that?" Arthur Cullen asked, though it was not a question. "Where does it come from, where does it go?"

Soon they were all skiing down the lake southwestwardly to South Cove, where they would break across country and up to the high ground. The lake was flat and effortless. They got into the track the boys made and slipped along as if on greased ways.

The snow was deeper than he had hoped it would be so that now, even with Timothy and Max exchanging the lead, he, and even the fourth man, Arthur, still had to stamp through new snow. Sometimes even the fourth man would still be knee deep in it. They took a number of small standing breaks, but after half an hour Timothy called a proper rest. Immediately he huddled with Max with compass and map; then he inspected the men.

"You're getting too wet," he told Arthur Cullen. "You should take off the parka as long as we're going up." He looked at his father. "How are you doing? How are you holding up?"

"How's our trail?" Philip said.

"Great. Right on. Straight as an arrow." He did not ask for agreement or support. He did not consult.

They started up again. Where the terrain grew steeper yet, and problematical, Timothy shouted back, "Only another ten minutes." But that was a trick, his own ploy that he had used on Timothy and his mother when it had been he who was leading. Ten minutes, he would encourage them, the young boy and the obliging wife, an urging promise even if a lie. And ten minutes more, and ten minutes more, until they were too angry with him to allow for the leak of self-pity that could scuttle them.

"Ten minutes more," Timothy shouted back. "For sure. We're almost there."

He let the rapture of the effort enfold him, let whatever care or caution had grown on him be scoured off. Here on the mountainside, kicking their way up, the boy deciding, nothing could remain of any other endeavor, any failure or success, any sweetness or any hurt.

He thought of his work. The hospital piece. He had invested heavily in it, but even if *The Atlantic* did not take it, there were other possibilities. He could easily cut it down or even shift the emphasis depending on the market. He knew how to cover himself that way. He would sell it, or a piece of it. Besides, he was hot. Two weeks ago he had sold a story to *Yankee*. And two weeks before that he had sold an article on Jerusalem artichokes to *Organic Gardening*. And the proposal for the biography of John Burroughs had been interestingly received at Hawthorne. If he got the contract for that, then that would pretty well settle him for the next eight months at least. And each day's mail brought him possibilities.

He had become what he had always wanted to be, just the kind of writer that he was, an eclectic wanderer, working at what he wanted or at what was available, a deft journeyman respected for his craft. Someone a contact in Albany might call upon to write a pamphlet about the state's water conservation efforts, someone friends in New York would ask for a profile piece on a ballerina or a scientist or a famous judge, a piece on wine or movies or travel.

The mortgage and insurance, the car and Timothy's teeth, the rebuilt furnace, the storm windows, the patched roof, the high assessment for the sewage hookup, the groceries and flour bought through the local coop as well as used clothing, but finally even the extravagant tape deck. He and Elaine had hammered it out: the small pleasant house he had built at the edge of the village, the sustaining garden, the warped but serviceable canoe. Even Timothy's college, coming soon, was half-prepared. They had managed and would manage. They had hammered it out of diligence and some spectres of lean defeat. Worry. Trouble. Words when no one would buy them.

He had not tried to do more. He had not tried to write a mighty novel or soaring stories or to etch the palimpsest of history with his words, to sear the image of his sensibility upon his age. He had dreamed no mightier dreams than the one he had come to live. Perhaps once. Perhaps, in the slight crease in his life just before Elaine and then Timothy, he had lingered in the chambers of his poetry and listened to his voice echo and reverberate, swell and then recede into the far, measureless caverns of the human mystery. For a time he thought he might go after his voice, follow it wherever it might go, into the vaulted dark. But he had married. The small crease was pulled smooth, and his life had been seamless, if not always firm, ever since.

Now on the flank of Garnet Hill, whatever he thought—thinking itself—was emptied of its life. The flesh of his thinking was absorbed in the pureness of the labored climbing, just as late yesterday the heavy air and toneless light had absorbed the day. His thoughts were like the delicate structures of small bleached sea creatures, the calcified skeletons, spiked and hollowed and convoluted or decorated with spicules and knobs. He looked at them all like specimens, as if they were ideas that could have belonged to anyone—as if they were arrangements in a museum, *examples* of thought, but not of the living. He felt nothing for them. He felt only the fullness of the relentless effort of climbing, the peacefulness that we imagine about obliteration, the climbing out of ourselves, beyond ourselves, free of our bodies, the spirit hovering free and clean above the panting machine of sinew and bone.

"We're here," Timothy yelled back down at them.

"We're here," Max yelled. His father was last. In his climbing he had escaped nothing. In his need to finish the last yards of the climb and be done with it, he had slipped continually and had fallen twice. He reached them at last, snow drenched and without enchantment.

"So what's 'here'?" Arthur said.

"We're here. We're at the top of the trail. We go down from here into North Mine and then down that to the lodge. It's down all the way from here, Poppy," Max said.

"Yeah, you could *roll* down from here and still get back," Timothy said.

"Yeah," Max said. "And he might!" They howled at that, bayed at the moon, full and pale and already risen even in the bright day.

"Humpty Dumpty," Timothy said.

"Humpty BUMPty," Max said.

"Humpty bumpity."

"Humpty bumpity bumpity bumpity bumpity."

They were not on the highest ridge of the mountain, not at the summit, but they were in the upper region that creates its own weather conditions. From where they stood they could see across small valleys and gullies where a dozen snow squalls whirled in place, little cyclonic oddities not fifty feet across. And where the mountain turned its bulk enough to miss the winter sun, miniature glaciers had formed, blue ice that would last until July, scooping out rocks into knife-edged cirques. They were in the region where the mountain made its own wind even when there was no wind lower. Already they were stiffening in it.

"Let's go," Timothy said.

"Let's go, Poppy," Max said to his father.

"We just got up here," Arthur said. "We just got here. I need something to eat. Who brought the cocoa?"

"*You* just got here, Poppy."

"Just wait a minute. Just wait, that's all." The wind had stiffened him, and the climbing and falling had made him taut with the expectation of fatigue. But he could not hold them. They could not hold themselves.

"After you, my dear Alphonse," Timothy said.

"No. After you, my dear Alphonse."

"No, no. After *you*."

"No, no, no. After *you*."

In a giggling burst they clattered against each other, jostling for the trail head.

"Humpity dumpity," Timothy shouted, reaching it first.

"Humpity bumpity bumpity, Poppy," Max shouted, following Timothy.

Philip listened to their voices disappear. They were gone nearly at once. The trail down was more quickly steep then he had thought.

The trail was ungroomed. The snowmobile with the heavy snow dredge behind it had not run over it, packing and leveling out the worst bumps. Perhaps too few used these upper trails for the lodge crew to bother with them. None of the deep pits had been filled with snow by a work crew. But even under better conditions the trail was only a narrow slash through the woods, the old trace of a logging road when horses had been used to skid out the second- or even third-growth timber. But what had worked for the deliberate horses against the pitch of the frozen mountain, with skidders hauling down on the heavy oak brakes, was diabolical for men.

The grade was just steep enough to cause a buildup to a difficult speed where the trail switched back on a hard angle, left or right. Worse than the humped and pocked and rutted surface was the jagged shape of the trail. At every turn you either swept by it into the deep, dead end of snow and fell and then worked your way back up to the turn; or you fell on purpose, sat down on your skis until you stopped and then walked back to the turn and walked through it. Or you tried to ski it, taking the curve as in a downhill race—but when you missed that way, you fell in a twisting roll, ploughing into the snow and maybe into buried branches or rocks. The snow would ram itself down the neck of your parka and into your mittens. Your face would burn and grow numb.

In twenty minutes Philip and Arthur had not descended very far. They had gone badly over the rough trail, without any ease or grace. The turns were nearly impossible for them; too soon they were battered and weary.

"It's crazy," Arthur said. "Absolutely nuts. This isn't a proper trail. This isn't a cross-country trail. This is a crime. The sons of bitches should be arrested for calling this a trail!"

"Eat some candy," Philip said.

"I don't want any candy. I'm sick from the goddamn candy. I want a goddamn martini this big, and a big goddamn fireplace to drink it next to."

But they were still in the private upper regions of the mountain.

"Come on." Philip stood up. He helped Arthur to stand. "This is no trail."

But where was the argument that this was not a trail? Timothy and Max were not here, stumbling and cold. So what could be said? That it was a trail for those who could survive it but not for those who might not?

Philip did better now, but not yet well. He tried to take the inevitability of the speed with him into the curve. He tried not to hold back but to throw himself, even against his will, into the force. He tried to relinquish his will to it. If the angle was favorable and he could do it, at the very edge of choice, he would leap *into* the more dangerous attitude and come through it. That was the elating trick: to defeat the danger by danger, to avoid the limits by going beyond them. It was exactly what the boys could do, not because of quicker motor reflexes or greater stores of energies, but because they could not imagine catastrophes like mortgages and dental bills and editors. And time. Deadlines.

Philip pounded through a turn so hard that it actually bent uphill again, only to snap him down like a whip even more quickly into another curve which he barreled out of like a rattling bobsled, faster and faster. He could go all the way down just as the boys had, like a blur through the menace of branches and trees only three or four feet away on each side. He could make it, but only if he would plunge into the speed itself, into the danger, into the descent, faster and faster until he became one with it.

But he could not. As soon as he considered his mounting speed, as soon as he calculated his approach to the turn shooting at him, he fell in a hard and daunting tumble.

When he had fallen at the top of his run, he had plunged his left hand through a crusting of snow hard and sharp as quartz, sharp enough to rip through his lightweight ski gloves. He saw his hand, the slit skin. The blood. The ice had anesthetized even as it cut; he felt no pain. The blood had oozed and spread into the glove and already had started to congeal.

Arthur reached him in a first glare of panic.

"I'm going to walk down. I'm taking off my skis. I'll walk it."

"No," Philip said. "You'll sink in. Stay on the skis."

"I *can't* stay on the skis. That's the point."

"It gets easier," Philip promised. "Ten, maybe fifteen more minutes of this and it starts to level out. I remember the map. Fifteen minutes, that's all. And we're below the wind now. See?"

"Where are the kids?" Arthur said. "We should have stayed together. You should always stay together. This goddamn trail."

But they could not have stayed together. The young, so lightly wounded that they cannot know it, speed on more and more quickly into the constant light, and those who are firmly lost have no claim on them. Philip sideslipped and edged down the trail, setting a pattern for Arthur to follow. He thought of the sleek boys by now probably back at the lodge, already planning tomorrow's assault. They had found a spur of path up to the summit itself, hardly more than an animal trail. Tomorrow, in one long run, the boys would swoop down from the very summit of Garnet, down Sawmill and over the link to North Mine, past the lodge without stopping, faster and faster like great archangels plummeting, the wind streaming through their singing pinions, down to the lake. Immaculate and steady, for a moment they would be borne up by an infinite mercy until, in another moment, high above some steeplechase we dare, doubt cracks us and we fall.

Dominion

In a moment, the twinkling of an eye, at the last trump: for the
trumpet shall sound, and the dead shall be raised incorruptible,
and we shall be changed.

I Corinthians 15:52

He played absently with the tiny party hat in his hand, a hat such
as a leprechaun in a movie cartoon might wear, a truncated cone
of metallic green paper with a flat silver brim and a black paper
buckle. He pulled at the thin rubber band that would hold the hat
in place and listened carefully to what the men were explaining.
Sometimes he would nod in comprehension. Last night he and
Sandra had gone to the Balmuth's New Year's Eve party. And now,
January the first, suddenly a lifetime later, he listened to the two
men, the accountant and the lawyer, explain what had happened.

What had happened was that Poverman & Charney, a small
manufacturer of lightweight women's clothing, was ruined, em-
bezzled into insolvency by Charney, who even now sat in Florida
in the noonday sun. Morton Poverman sat here, at his chilling
dining room table cloaked with the fabric of his loss, the neat
stacks of paper—bills, letters, invoices, bank statements, memo-
randa, and packets of canceled checks—that chronicled Charney's
wretched course, his wicked testament.

Poverman said, "And all this could have happened without my
knowing? Amazing."

In a corner off from the table, Poverman's wife, Sandra, sat in a
stuffed chair with her right leg raised up on a ottoman. Her leg, up
to the middle of the calf, was in a cast, her ankle broken. "Oh,"

she said like a moan, a curse, a threat. "Oh, God." It was all she could say now, though later, Poverman knew, she would say more, her vehemence strident, hot, and deep. For twenty years she had disliked Phil Charney, distrusted him always, his flamboyance, his fancy women and his fancy ways, the frivolous instability of his unmarried state. And now to be right! To be helplessly confirmed! She put her head back against the chair and closed her eyes as she clogged with rage nearly to fainting. "Oh, God."

"Not so amazing," the accountant snapped. "You never looked at the books. You never asked a question." Friedsen slapped at some figures on a pad before him. "Five thousand dollars for the material for the chemises? When is the last time you made a chemise? Who buys chemises anymore? And this?" He looked down at the pad. "The bias tapes? Forty cases? And here," he jabbed at the entry with his finger, his nail piercing the numbers like the beak of a ravening bird. "The printing bill on the new boxes? You weren't suspicious of that?" Friedsen was angry. He had done their books from the start, had managed them well. And now he held them in his hands like smudged ashes. Like dirt. Like an affront. If one was a thief, then the other was a fool.

"I never looked at the books," Poverman told him, though Friedsen knew that already, knew everything. "If I had looked, so what would I have known? I did the selling, Philly did the rest. For twenty-five years it worked OK."

"The bastard," Friedsen said.

Poverman could not find his own anger. Perhaps he was still too startled. What Phil Charney had done he had done quickly, in less than a year altogether, but conclusively in the last quarter before the Christmas season, when their money moved about most rapidly and in the largest amounts. Friedsen, for his own orderly reasons, liked to see his client's fiscal shape at the end of the calendar year. He had gotten to Poverman & Charney two days ago and, hour by hour, he had tumbled ever more quickly through the shreds that Charney had made of the once solid company. Friedsen had gone to no New Year's Eve party. And this morning he had pulled the lawyer, Kuhn, to this dreadful meeting. It had not taken him long to explain and demonstrate the bankruptcy and its cause.

Now Kuhn explained the rest, the mechanism of foreclosure and collection, the actual bankruptcy petition to the courts, the appointment of the referee, the slim possibility of criminal action against Charney. He went on, but to Poverman the intricacies of his disaster, like the details of his success, were equally abstractions. He could not contain them. He could understand the results, of course; he could understand the purposes and conclusions. Consequences. But he had always been the man in front, the one to whom you spoke when you called Poverman & Charney. Morton Poverman, a man of good will and even humor who had put in his working years directly, flesh on flesh, voice against voice, eye to eye. Let Friedsen and Kuhn do what must be done in their rigorous and judicial way. But let him do what he could do in his.

"So what's left?" he asked, first to one and then the other. "Anything?"

Of the business there was not much. He would lose the factory and everything in it and connected to it, including the dresses, housecoats, and nightgowns already on the racks. There were two outlet stores. The largest, the newer store in Fairlawn Shopping Mall, he would have to close; the older store, in the business strip just off North Broadway, he could probably keep. Where he and Phil had begun.

Personally, there was the paid-up life insurance, fifty thousand. That was safe. There was also about twenty thousand in cash. There were things like the cars and all that was in the house. The house itself might be a question. Kuhn said the house would depend on too many variables to discuss now. And there was the trust fund for Robert's education. Twenty-five thousand dollars. Nothing could touch that. There were some small investments, mostly stocks. Those would probably have to be called in, for one reason or another. For one bill or another—Friedsen's perhaps, or Kuhn's. Or merchandise for the store. At this point who could say?

"So? That's it?"

"That's about it," Kuhn said.

"Well, it's not nothing, is it?" Poverman said.

"No," Kuhn said. "It's not nothing."

Sandra Poverman sobbed high and quietly, still unable to open her eyes to what she would have to look at forever after.

When the men left he did some small figuring of his own. Immediately there would be no Florida vacation this winter. Perhaps he would sell one car. The membership in the country club? What did he need that for, he didn't play golf. He started to write down numbers—mortgage payment, property tax, homeowner's insurance, the car payments, but after these he could not say. He did not know what his heating bill was, his electricity, food, clothing. And the rest. Did Sandra? Did anyone in this house know such things? Probably not. He had earned, each year a little more, and in the last five years nearly, though not quite, a lot. Yesterday the future was all before him, various with pleasures just about to come within his grasp: the long-planned trips to Europe, to South America the year after that, Hawaii. The house in the semi-retirement village at Seadale, a hundred miles north of Miami. Gone. Today only the future itself was waiting, empty and dangerous. The little store on North Broadway with the old lighting fixtures and the cracked linoleum flooring from twenty-five years ago. That was waiting.

He had earned, they all had spent what they needed, and each year they had needed a little more. So now they would need less. They would make an accommodation. Tomorrow he would go to the outlet store and take stock and make arrangements. Begin.

He was fifty-three.

The phone rang. It was Phil Charney calling from Miami. He knew Friedsen would find him in the year-end audit.

"Morty, this is Phil. You know why I'm calling?"

"Friedsen was here. Just now. And Kuhn. They just left."

"Morty, this is so terrible, I can't say how terrible."

Sandra stiffened. "That's him?" she hissed. He nodded. "Give me." She motioned the phone to her. "Give me. I'll tell him something. I'll tell that filth something. Give me. Give me." She waved for the phone, her voice rising. He covered the mouthpiece. She tried to stand up.

"Morty, I'm sitting here weeping. I didn't sleep all night. Not for two nights. Not for three nights. I couldn't help it. I still can't.

She wants and wants and I must give. *Must!* Who knows where it ends? There's not so much money I can go on like this. Then what? But what can I do? *Morty,* what can I do, kill myself?''

"No, no, of course not.''

He scrambled for his outrage like a weapon, but a weapon with which to defend himself, not to attack. He was embarrassed for the man sobbing at the other end of the line, for his agony. When he summoned his hatred for protection, it would not come. But he had always lacked sufficient imagination, and what he felt now was more the loss of his lifelong friend, the swoop and gaiety of his presence as he would click about the factory, kidding the women on the machines, hassling in mocking fights the blacks on the loading platforms. He had even picked up enough Spanish to jabber back at the volatile Puerto Ricans. Even the Puerto Ricans Phil could make laugh and work.

That would be gone. And the flitting elegance, the Cadillacs and the women. The clothing and the jewelry. The flights to anywhere, to Timbuktu. He would miss the women. They were an excitement, these strenuous pursuits of Phil Charney's, these expensive pursuits. He was a tone, an exuberant vibrato that pushed into and fluttered the lives of anyone near him. Battered floozies or sometimes women much younger, but often enough recently divorced or widowed women ready at last for madder music, headier wine. Sandra Poverman condemned it, but her husband could afford his own small envy, safe enough within his wife's slowly thickening arms to tease her with his short-reined lust.

That would be gone. Tomorrow he would go to work, as he had known he would even before Friedsen, but now in silence with no edge of scandal or tightly fleshed surprise.

"Filth! Murderer!'' Sandra shouted into the phone. She had gotten up and hobbled over to him. "Liar! Dog!''

"She's right, Morty. She's right. I'm no better than a murderer.''

"No. Stop this, Phil. Get a hold.''

"Die!'' Sandra screamed. "Die in hell! Bastard! Scum!'' She pulled at the phone in his hand, but he forced her back.

"Oh, Morty, Morty, what I've done to you! Oh, Morty, forgive me.''

"Yes, Phil. OK. I do." He hung up before either could say more.

What more? That time had come to take away their life together, abandoning Phil Charney more severely than himself? If he had said that, would he be certain enough what he meant? That only the sorrow was left, enough of that to go around for them all, so what did the rest matter?

"What?" Sandra demanded. "What did he want? 'I do,' you said. You 'do' what?" He told her. She screamed, raised her fists to her ears to block his words, but too late. She fell against him, staggered by the shaking that was bringing down upon her the castles they had built. And now he had even taken from her the solid and pure energy of revenge.

The North Broadway store had made economic sense as an outlet for the factory, a nice way of taking some retail profit right off the top. But without the factory as the primary supplier, the store was just another women's clothing store, competition everywhere. That situation would be impossible. But Morton Poverman had his accrued advantages from twenty-five years in both ends of the business. He knew enough to know where he could get overruns, returns, seconds from other manufacturers, small producers such as he had been. What credit he needed he could still get from them, at least with some cash down.

By the end of January he could at least begin to think seriously about his spring line; various enough and inexpensive as it was, he had a chance to exist. Not much more. Already the stock was coming into the storeroom faster than he could handle it. Still, that was not so bad; better more than not enough. He would put in the time to inventory and price and mark it all.

In January he had let go all the workers in the store, three of them, and handled the front himself. Only on Saturday, dashing back and forth from customer to cash register, was it too difficult. The stock he worked on at night. At first until nine o'clock, and now until midnight. But it was coming together, the store brightening with variety and loading up with goods. And people were still shopping downtown, he could tell. He would get by on his low pricing and his long hours. And now he was bringing in a whole line of Playtex girdles and bras, all kinds of pantyhose and lingerie. In a year maybe he would bring in sewing materials, fabrics, patterns. In a year. Or two.

It was easier to say that twenty-five years ago, when there was still a year or two or three or five to invest. And two of them to do it. But he could say it now nonetheless, again and alone. His flame burned, steadily if low, even by the end of January when, like fuel for the flame, Bobby's Scholastic Aptitude Test scores arrived: 690 in Verbal, 710 in Math. Fuel enough. Then Morton Poverman would lean back into the large cardboard boxes under the dim, bare-bulbed lighting of the storeroom with his supper sandwich and the last of his thermos of coffee and think that though he was bone-weary and hard-pressed, he was not without intelligent purpose and a decent man's hope. More he did not ask. Or need.

February, March—a time for clinging to the steep, roughly grained rock face of his endeavor, seeking the small, icy handholds, the cracks and fissures of little victories by which to lever himself up an inch: he picked up one hundred assorted dusters for nearly nothing, garbage from South Korea with half their buttons gone. He would replace the buttons. Kurtlanger's, the largest women's clothing store in the area, was dropping its entire line of women's nylons. It was not worth the bother to Kurtlanger's to supply the relatively few women who still wore separate stockings; it was all pantyhose now. For Poverman the bother could become his business. He stocked the nylons and put an ad in the newspaper saying so. Seeds for springtime. He put money into a new floor, found bags in Waltham, Massachusetts, at a 10 percent saving, joined the Downtown Merchants' Association lobbying for increased side-street lighting and greater police surveillance. He checked three times a day the long-range weather reports. Would winter freeze him shut, March blow his straw house down?

At first Sandra had gone mad with anger, calling everyone to behold her suffering. She called her friends and relatives, Charney's friends and relatives, the police. Worse than the stunning death of a loved one in a car crash or by quick, violent blooming of a cancer in the lymph nodes, which let you curse God and be done with it, what Charney had done to her was an unshared burden, separate from life and others' fates, and unsupportable for being so. If we all owe life a death and perhaps even pain, certainly we do not owe it bankruptcy and humiliation. She cried out, howled, keening in the ancient way of grief and lamentation.

And then she dropped into silence like a stone.

She would hardly speak to him, as if his failure to share her intensity of anger had separated them. Or speak to anyone. She grew hard and dense with her misery, imploded beneath the gravity of her fury and chagrin. At first she had fought with her simple terrifying questions: Who could she face? What was the rest of her life to be like? But then, far beyond her questions, she grew smaller until at the last she atomized into the vast unspecific sea of justice and worth, and there she floated, like zero.

Late at night Poverman would come home and get into bed beside her and chafe her arms and rub her back. Sometimes he would kiss her gently on the neck, as she had always liked. But she was wood. Still, he would talk to her, tell her the good things that were happening, describe his incremental progress, prepare her for the future. But she would not go with him. The future, like her past, had betrayed her, had disintegrated. She would trust no future again.

Robert Poverman said to his father, ''I'll come in after school. You'll show me how to mark the clothing, and that will be a help.''

''No,'' his father said. ''By the time you come in after school, get downtown, it would already be late. What could you do in an hour?''

''What do you mean, 'an hour'? I'd work with you at night. I'd come home with you. If I helped, then we'd both get home earlier.''

''No. Absolutely not. You're in school. You do the school, I'll do the business. In the summer, we'll see. Not now, Sonny. Not now.''

''Are you kidding, Dad? School's over. I'm a second semester senior. It's all fun and games, messing around. It's nothing.''

"So do fun and games. Mess around. That's part of school, too. Next year you'll be in college, with no messing around. And what about your activities, the Photography Club, the Chess Club, Student Council? Your guitar? And soon it's track season. So what about track?" Poverman knew it all, remembered everything.

"Dad, listen. I'm a third-string miler; sometimes they don't even run me. I struggle to break six minutes. And the clubs are strictly baloney. Nothing. Believe me, *nothing*. Let me help you, please. Let me *do* something."

"No. *No*. If you want to do something, Sonny, do school, *all* of it just the way you always did. Do it the way you would have before . . . *this*." He smeared his hand in the air.

His son took his hand out of the air and kissed it. "OK, Dad," he said softly. "OK. And I'll pray for you, too."

That night, turning the handle of the machine that ground out the gummed pricing tags, Poverman recalled what his son had said, that he would pray for him. The machine clicked on: size, stock number, price. What could that mean? But Poverman had enough to think about without adding prayer. He had ten crates of L'eggs to unpack by morning, two dozen bathrobes that had arrived that day without belts, and all the leather accessories that he still had to tag. He turned the crank faster.

March, and now, somehow, April. Already the first wave of Easter buying had lapped at his shore, eroded slightly the cloth of his island. Good. Let it all be washed away in a flood of gold. Poverman was working harder than ever, but accomplishing more. The hard, heavy work was mostly done; there was a shape to everything now, his possibilities limited but definite, and definite perhaps because they were limited. So be it. He had started in quicksand and had built his island. The rest now was mostly up to the weather and the caprice of the economy. At least it was out of the hands of men like Phil Charney.

Poverman seldom thought of Phil, even though he had to meet often enough with Friedsen and Kuhn. He had even made a joke once that he had to work for Charney twice, before and after. Friedsen had not laughed. But what did it matter? What mattered was what *could* matter.

It was six o'clock. He walked about in the crisp store, straightening a few boxes, clothes loosely strewn in bins, the merchandise hanging on the racks. Tonight, for the first time in months, he was closing now. Tonight he was going home early. To celebrate. Let the three hundred pairs of slippers from the Philippines wait. Let the gross of white gloves wait. Tonight he was going home to celebrate. Today, all on the same day, Robert Poverman had been accepted at Yale, Cornell, and the State University of New York at Binghamton, a university center. He had until May 15 to make his decision and send in his deposit. They would talk about it tonight. And everything.

Poverman turned out all the lights after checking the locks on the back door. He walked out, pulling the door closed and double locking it. He looked up at the sign recently painted on the door, the new name he had decided upon: The Fashion Center. Nothing too fancy. Nothing too smart. But what did he need with fancy or smart? He had Robert Poverman of Yale or Cornell. *That* was fancy. *That* was smart.

After supper Poverman spread out the various catalogs and forms and descriptive literature from the three colleges. He added clippings from magazines and newspapers. They had seen most of it before, when Robert had applied, but now it was to be examined differently as one seriously considered the tangibilities of life in Harkness Memorial Hall or Mary Donlon Hall. This material was what they had from which to read the auguries of Robert Poverman's future. Even Sandra leavened as they discussed (As always. Again.) what he would study. Which school might be best for what. Neither Poverman nor his wife knew how to make their comparisons. It would, now as before, be their son's choice. But who could refrain from the talking? The saying of such things as law or medicine or physics or international relations? Poverman again looked up the size of the libraries. Yale: 6,518,848. Cornell: 4,272,959. SUNY at Binghamton: 729,000. 6,518,848 books. How could he imagine that? Still, it was one measure. But what did Robert Poverman want? His interests were so wide, his accomplishments so great, what could he *not* decide for? What could he not cast for and catch?

They drank tea and talked. In two days Sandra would go for a small operation on the ankle to adjust a bone that had drifted slightly. Even with his medical coverage it would cost him a thousand dollars. But OK. Of course. Let her walk straight. Let their life go on. He had hoped she would be able to help him in the store now that the Easter push was happening, but instead he had hired someone part time.

He looked at the pictures in the college catalogs, the jungle of glass tubes in the laboratories, the pretty girls intensely painting things on large canvases, the professor standing at the blackboard filled with lines and numbers and signs like a magical incantation, smiling young men like Robert flinging frisbees across the wide commons, the view of Cayuga Lake, the wondrous glowing cube of the Beinecke Library at Yale (*another* library, a *special* library for the rare books alone). Yale. Yale began to creep into Morton Poverman's heart. He would say nothing. What did he know? It was up to Robert. But he hoped for Yale. 6,518,848 books.

"I don't know," Robert said. "What's the rush?" He turned to Sandra.

"This is an important decision, right? And he's got a month. Think about it, that's the smart thing," he said to his son. "Sure. Don't jump before you look." He gathered up the evidence of what was to come, the scattered materials about one of Robert Poverman's schools, and put it all back into the reddish-brown paper portfolio. He took the letters of acceptance and the letters to be returned with the deposit and put them elsewhere. He wished he could have sent one back in the morning with a check enclosed, a down payment on his son's happiness, a bond, a covenant.

That night in bed he held his wife's hand.

"Which do you like?" he asked.

"Cornell, I think."

"Not Yale? Why not Yale?"

"The bulldog," she said. "It's so ugly. What kind of animal is that for a school?"

The weather was balmy, good for light cotton prints. Easter did well by him, and spring, too. Business was coursing through the veins of the store. Sandra's ankle was fixed for good now, mending correctly, though she would still need more weeks of resting it. This Sunday he had asked Robert to come to the store to help him catch up on some stock work. Also he wanted to describe what Robert would do that summer. Robert would work in the store and his pay, except for some spending money, would be put into a bank account for his use in college. Today Poverman would push his son, slightly, toward his decision. Time was now growing short: ten days until the deadline. He would like to have this settled.

At three o'clock they sat down to some sandwiches that Sandra had packed for them

"So? What do you think?" he asked his son. "Can you last the summer? Listen, this is the easy part. The stock don't talk back. The stock don't complain. You think you can explain to a size 12 lady why she don't fit into a size 10 dress? Hah? Let me tell you, sweetheart, everything to know is not in books." Then he reached across and stroked his son's softly stubbled cheek. His oldest gesture. "But Sonny, all of this is nothing to know. What you're going to learn, compared to this, you could put all this into a little nutshell." Then, "Did you choose a college yet?"

Robert Poverman said, "I don't know."

"There's only ten days," his father said. "What can you know in ten more days that you don't know already? What do you want to know? Who can you ask? Sonny, maybe you think you have to be certain. Well, let me tell you, you can't be certain of nothing. And with any one of these schools, you can't go so far wrong. You can't lose."

"It's about college. I'm not so sure about that."

His father did not understand.

"Maybe college isn't for me. Just yet, anyway. I don't know."

"Know?" his father said. "Know what. What is there to know? You think you want *this*?" he indicated the store around them. "Maybe you want to go into the army? Shoot guns? Maybe you want to be a fireman and ride on a red truck?"

"Don't be angry, Dad. Please."

But it wasn't anger ballooning in Morton Poverman now; it was panic.

"Then what are you talking about? *What* don't you know? You go to college to find out what you don't know. Ah," it occurred to him, "it's the money. Is that it? You're worried about the money, about me and your mother. But I told you, the money is already there. Twenty-five thousand and that will make interest. Plus a little more I've got. Plus what you'll earn. Don't worry about the money. I swear to you, your mother and I are going to be OK that way. Look, look. The store is working out, Sonny."

"Dad, it's not that. Maybe there's another way." They were silent.

"So?" Poverman finally asked. "What other way?"

"I've been thinking about religion." He looked at his father evenly. "There's a religious retreat down at this place in Nyack this summer, from the middle of July to the middle of August. I think maybe I should go there." He looked down, away from his reflection in his father's brightening eyes.

"Why?"

"Yes, *why*. I need to find out the meaning of things. Not *what* I want to do or where I want to go to college, but *why*. Is that unreasonable?"

But what did Morton Poverman know about reasonableness? What he knew about was hanging on, like a boxer after he has been hit very hard.

"So what has this to do with college? Why can't I send in the deposit?"

"I might not go to college right away. I can't honestly say now. Or I might not want to go to one of those colleges. Where I was accepted. I might find out that I want to go to a . . . a religious type of college. I just don't know. I've got to think about it. I don't want you wasting the money. If I change my mind, I can probably still get into a good college somewhere."

"Money again," Poverman roared. He stood. "I'm telling you, money is shit! I know. I've lost money before. That's nothing!"

Driving home from the store Robert told his father that for the past six months he had been attending weekly meetings for high school age people organized by the Society of the Holy Word. Driving down Pearl Street, he pointed to a store with many books in the window and the name of the organization neatly lettered on the panes.

"So everybody's in business," Poverman said as he drove by. "Do they belong to the Downtown Merchants' Association?"

"They're not selling," his son said.

"Aren't they? So what's that, a church?"

"No, Dad. It isn't a business and it isn't a church. It's a place for people to meet to discuss things."

"Yeah? Like what?"

"Religion, the meaning of life, ethical conduct. The Bible, mostly. The Bible as the word of God."

"Is that right? The Bible tells you what college to go to? Yale or Cornell? Amazing. I never knew. But then, there's so much I don't know."

"Dad, please. Don't be angry. Don't be bitter."

"No? So what should I be, happy? For eighteen years I'm thinking Chief Justice of the Supreme Court and now my son tells me he's thinking of becoming a monk. Wonderful. Terrific." He drove faster.

"Ah, Daddy, come on. It's not that way at all. We sit and talk about how religion can give a full and wonderful meaning to our lives. It's raised some important questions for me about my future. And it's offered some possible answers and solutions."

"Solutions? Why? You've got problems?"

"We've all got problems, Daddy."

"Like?"

"Like our souls," Robert Poverman said. "Like the fate of our immortal souls."

"Souls? *Souls?* You're eighteen and you're worried about your soul? What about your body?"

But his son closed down then, as did he. Each caught the other's orbit, but silently now, and as awesomely distant as Venus from Pluto. And what could the earthbound Morton Poverman breathe in such empty space?

"Yes? Can I help you?" the tall man asked. He was very clean, scrubbed pink and white. He did not seem to need to shave, his skin as smooth as thin polished stone, nearly translucent. His steel-grey hair was combed straight back. He wore small octagonal rimless glasses.

"Just looking," Poverman said. He walked about in the converted store. Converted to what? All he saw were arrangements of books with such titles as *Satan in the Sanctuary* and *Which Will You Believe?* There were piles of small folded tracts and pamphlets on colored paper, pink, green, blue. Newspapers called the *New Word Times* and *Revelation Tribune*. On the walls were poster-sized photographs of people, mostly healthy young people, working at good deeds in foreign countries, in ghettos, in hospitals, in old folks' homes. Even Poverman could quickly see that the young people in the photographs were shining with pleasure in the midst of the misery and needs they were serving, gleaming and casting light that warmed and illuminated the rheumy-eyed old woman in the wheelchair; the bloated, scabbed children in the jungle clearing; the slit-eyed hoodlum sucking deeply on his joint of dope. All down the wall—growing, building, feeding, helping. Hallelujah.

Past the main room, behind a partition, was another room. He turned and walked back to the pink and white man.

"I'm Morton Poverman," he said, and put out his hand.

"I'm George Fetler," the pink and white man took his hand.

"I've got a son, Robert Poverman. He comes here."

"Oh, yes. Robert. A wonderful boy. Brilliant, absolutely brilliant. I'm very pleased to meet you. You must be very proud of such a son."

But Poverman did not have time for this playing. Even now, four blocks away in his own store, United Parcel trucks would be arriving with goods he must pay for, and he had not yet made the bank deposit that would cover them. Francine Feynmen (now working full time) would be on two customers at once (or worse, none), and the phone would ring with the call from Philadelphia about the slightly faded Orlon sweaters. And what had he come here for, this man's opinions?

"Yes," Poverman said. "Proud." But he did not know what to say, what to do. What he *wanted* to do was dump five gallons of gasoline over everything—the books, the newspapers, the green pamphlets—and put a match to it. But there were too many other empty storefronts downtown for that to matter.

George Fetler said, "You're probably here because you're worried about Robert."

"Yes. That's right. Exactly." Poverman beat down the small loop of gratitude.

"Robert's such a thoughtful fellow. He's quite uncertain about college now, about his future. I suppose you and Mrs. Poverman must be concerned."

"Yes," Poverman said again, eagerly, even before he could stop himself. This guy was smooth. He was a salesman, all right, as soft as Poverman was hard.

"You're probably upset with the Society of the Holy Word, too."

Poverman clamped his lips but nodded.

"You must think we've poisoned your son's mind."

Poverman nodded again.

"Let's sit down, Mr. Poverman, and let me tell you about us. Briefly. You're probably anxious to get back to your business."

Oh, terrific. All his life Morton Poverman had wished he could have been so smooth with customers—buying, selling, complaints, but with him it had always been a frontal attack. A joke, a little screaming or a quick retreat into a deal for 20 percent off. But never like this, quiet, slick as oil, full of probabilities, the ways so easily greased. Yes, yes, where do I sign?

George Fetler took him into the back room. Half the room was set up as for a small class, rows of metal chairs facing a small table and blackboard. The other half of the room contained soft chairs drawn around in a circle. They sat there.

George Fetler described simply and directly what the Society of the Holy Word did as far as Robert Poverman was concerned. On Thursday evening it conducted, right here, right in these soft chairs, discussions about religion generally, Christianity specifically, and most of all the idea that the Bible was the exact word of God.

"That's it?" Poverman asked.

"Let's be frank. Let *me* be frank. If you believe the Bible is the exact word of God, then that can certainly raise some important questions about how you lead your life henceforth. I think this is what has happened to Robert. He came to us six months ago with two friends. I'm sure he came because his two friends, already Christians, wanted him to come. Like many before him, he came more as a lark, skeptical and doubting. But he read the Bible and he discussed what he read; the questions arose, Mr. Poverman, they just arose. And Mr. Poverman, I just wish you could see him, his openness, his honesty, his intelligence. It is very gratifying. Very." Fetler sat back and locked his hands together in front of him.

"You'll pardon me for asking," Poverman asked anyway, "but how does all this get paid for?"

George Fetler smiled, unlocked his hands, and stood up. "Here. This will explain it in detail." He went out to the tables in front and returned with a booklet. "This will tell you what you probably want to know, including a financial statement. The Society of the Holy Word is but one arm of the Church of the Resurrection, Incorporated. We're based in Chicago. We've got our printing operation there and headquarters for our evangelical units. The church also has two colleges, one in San Diego, the other. . . ."

"In Nyack?"

"Yes. Has Robert mentioned that? He's thinking of going on our summer retreat there."

"But sooner or later, it all comes down to them—what do you call it?—coming out for Jesus? Right?"

"One need not declare for Christ, but that is what we hope will happen." George Fetler and Morton Poverman were coming closer now to what they thought of each other. "Yes. That is what we hope and pray for."

"Why?"

"It is," George Fetler said, not such a soft guy anymore (no sale here), "the only way to avoid the everlasting torments of Hell."

Morton Poverman had never been able to handle the Christian's Hell. It looked to him like the answer to everything and to nothing. And what did they need it for, this endless knife at the throat? Besides, about Hell—here now, right away—he had his own ideas. No, not ideas. Necessities.

His week went on, all his life a tactical adventure now, no crease in it without its further unexpected bend, no crack that might not open up suddenly into an abyss from which he could not scramble back. This is what he slept with now. Battle. War.

On Thursday evening at seven o'clock he went to the discussion meeting at 183 Pearl Street, the Society of the Holy Word. He had studied. From the array of pamphlets and tracts on the tables in the Society's store he had selected copiously. And he had read them, late at night in the back of the store, later than ever, he had read slowly in the bad light, bent to this new labor as the unopened cartons piled up on each other and each morning Francine Feynman would complain of empty this and unreplaced that.

The Bible says you have sinned!
Since all have sinned and fall short of the glory of God (Rom. 3:23)
The Bible says you deserve Hell!
For the wages of sin is death, but the free gift of God is eternal life in Christ Jesus our Lord (Rom. 6:23)
The Bible says you have a choice!
And if you be unwilling to serve the Lord, choose this day whom you will serve . . . (Joshua 24:15)
The Bible says Jesus died for you!
But God shows his love for us in that while we were yet sinners Christ died for us (Rom. 5:8)
The Bible says you must believe Jesus!
For, every one who calls upon the name of the Lord will be saved (Rom. 10:13)
The Bible says you have eternal life!
And this is the testimony, that God gave us eternal life, and this life is in his Son. He who has the Son has life. (I John 5:11–12)

Poverman got himself a Bible and checked it out. It was all there.

Ten people attended the Tuesday night meeting, all Robert's age or a little older, all regulars, except for the new member, Morton Poverman, who was introduced all around. Also attending were

George Fetler and the Reverend Julius Meadly, who more or less conducted things.

It went well enough. After Poverman explained that he had come out of interest in his son's interest and his talk with Mr. Fetler, the discussion picked up where, apparently, it had left off the preceding week.

The point of concern (always a tough one, Reverend Meadly told them) was whether those born before Christ (before, that is, the opportunity to receive Christ) would go to Hell. The Reverend drew the distinction between pagans, who had not had the chance to embrace Christ, and heathens, those born since Christ who did and do have the opportunity but reject it. Heathens were unquestionably doomed to Hell, but about pagans there was still some serious debate, for surely Abraham and the prophets were in Heaven already, and Moses as well as Adam.

They discussed at length the fairness of this, that those who had had no choice should be so grievously punished. The Reverend said that indeed the ways of the Lord were not always apparent to Man, and they were certainly unfathomable, but it did no good to question what was *not* going to happen to the pagans, and one should concentrate instead on the glory of what *was* going to happen to the saved. He concluded, "You know, sometimes I think that the last chapter and verse isn't completed. That on Judgment Day, God in his infinite wisdom and mercy will raise up even the unfortunate pagans." They closed on that high note.

Through the evening Robert Poverman had said nothing. Driving home he said, "What are you doing?"

"What do you mean?" his father said.

"You know what I mean. Why did you come tonight?"

"What's the matter, suddenly it's not a free country? A man can't worship how he wants anymore?"

"Cut it out, Dad. You know what I mean."

"You go to this place because you've got questions, right?" Poverman said. "Well, I've got questions too."

"Like what?"

"Like have you declared for Jesus, or whatever you call it?"

"No."

"Are you going to?"

"I don't know. I can't say."

"Do you believe in all that . . . stuff?"

"I think about it." They drove on in silence. "Are you going back? To another meeting?" Robert asked.

"Yeah. Sure. I still got my questions. What about you? Are you going back?"

Robert did not answer. "You're not sincere," he said.

But there, Morton Poverman knew, his son was wrong.

He hacked at his store and grew bleary with fatigue. What he sold in front he brought in through the back and touched everything once, twice, thrice in its passage. Slips, underwear, dresses, bandannas, now bathing suits and beach or pool ensembles. From passing over all that plastic, his fingertips were sanded as smooth as a safecracker's. And doggedly he studied the Word of the Lord. Bore up his wife. Bore his son.

At the second meeting that Morton Poverman attended, George Fetler understood. Robert Poverman, once so animated and involved, would not participate, not in the presence of his father. And the blunt intensity of his father's questions caused the Reverend Meadly to veer about, put his helm over frequently to avoid the jutting rocks of Morton Poverman's intent. Not that he was making an argument; he was polite enough, whatever that cost him. But his questions, they were so fundamental.

Almost all of the group had been together for months and had already covered the ecclesiastical ground that was new to him. It was not fair to the group to have to pause so often while the Reverend Meadly (the soul of patience) answered in detail what they all had heard and discussed before. This is what Fetler explained to Poverman after the meeting.

"You're throwing me out?" Poverman said. "You're telling me to go elsewhere with my soul in danger of eternal perdition?" He had studied well. He had the lingo, like in every line of work.

"No, no," Fetler said, growing more pink than ever. Close to him Poverman could see the blue fretwork of his veining. His whole face was like a stained-glass window. "That would be unthinkable, of course. What I had in mind was our Sunday afternoon group for older people." Poverman shook his head at Sunday afternoon. "Or private instruction," Fetler followed up. "Perhaps you could come to us, the Reverend Meadly or me, on another evening? Then we could give you a 'cram course,' so to speak?"

"OK," Poverman said. They agreed on Tuesday night.

On Tuesday night Poverman met with Reverend Meadly and after two hours of explaining—starting with Genesis (oh, it would be a long time before he would be able to rejoin the young group, already well into Corinthians), Poverman leaned back and said, "But it's all faith, isn't it? All this reasoning, all this explaining; if you've got faith, that's all that matters."

"Yes," the Reverend said. "Faith more than anything else."

"And if you get the faith, then what?"

"You must declare it. You must stand forth and join God through His Son, Jesus Christ."

"Yes, but how? I mean, could I just say it to you now? Is that enough? Would God know?"

"If you declare yourself through us, the Church of the Resurrection, there are certain formalities."

"A ceremony?"

"Yes, that's right. You must answer certain questions, take certain vows before a congregation."

"What about this?" Poverman produced one of the pamphlets that the Society of the Holy Word published. "Wherever I look, I'm always on trial. Some trial. Listen." He read the fiery indictment through to the end. " 'Verdict: Guilty as charged. Appeal: None. Sentence: Immediately eternal, conscious, tormenting, separational death in a burning lake of fire and brimstone.' "

"Well?" Reverend Meadly asked. Nothing else.

"So that's it for me? For Robert."

"Unless you embrace the Lord Jesus as your Savior, that is your fate and Robert's fate, yes."

"No either/or, huh?"

"Either Love or Damnation," Reverend Meadly said. Kindly.

On Thursday Poverman showed up at the meeting. Fetler called him aside. "I thought we agreed that you would work privately?"

"I wouldn't say a single word," Poverman promised. "I'll listen. I'll watch. I can learn a lot that way, and I won't interrupt. Not one word."

But there were no longer any words to say, for Morton Poverman had decided that at long last the time and event had come for God to stand forth and defend Himself, make good this terrible threat and vaunt or scram. He had paid enough with good faith and would not bargain now. He had reached his sticking price: take it or leave it. What was his, was his, and what belonged to his son, the legacy of his life, for all his—Poverman's—own clumsiness on this Earth, *that* he would not let be stolen easily. And whosoever should raise his hand or voice against his son must answer for that to him.

Thus girded, midway through the meeting Poverman suddenly stood up. The Reverend Meadly had just finished an intricate restatement of Paul's words: "In a moment, in the twinkling of an eye, at the last trump: for the trumpet shall sound, and the dead shall be raised incorruptible, and we shall be changed."

Poverman stood up and said: "Me, too. I have seen the way and the light. I want to declare for Jesus."

There was commotion.

"Mr. Poverman!" George Fetler said, standing too, quickly in his alarm.

"Now," Poverman said. "Right now. The spirit is in me." He stepped away from the group of seated young people and then turned to them. " 'Be ye followers of me, even as I also am of Christ,' " he intoned, trying to get it right. One of the group clapped. "I've been thinking and so this is what I want to do, thanks to Reverend Meadly." Reverend Meadly smiled, but Fetler curdled, his pink now blotched into redness.

"So what's next?" Poverman asked. "What have I got to do?"

There was a happy excitement in the young people at this immanence of spirit, all the thick words of the past months come true like a miracle. Fetler urged a later time, a more appropriate time for the declaration. "Now," Poverman insisted. "Between now and later, who knows what could happen? And *then* what about my soul?" He looked at Fetler. "Now."

Robert Poverman, stiff and frozen, watched his father don white robes (cotton/polyester—60/40, not silk) that drooped to the floor and take in either hand a large Bible and a heavy brass crucifix. The classroom was turned into a chapel, the lights dimmed. The Reverend Meadly took his place behind the table. From a drawer in the table he took out a paper.

"Wait," Poverman said. "I want my son Robert to stand next to me. He should see this up close." He motioned Robert to him.

The Reverend said, "You must be delivered to Christ by one who has already received Him. Robert has not yet."

"That's OK," Poverman said. "Let Mr. Fetler deliver me. I just want my son to stand by. This is a big thing for me." And so it was arranged, George Fetler, crimson and his eyes like thin slivers, on Poverman's right, Robert Poverman, cast into numb darkness, on his father's left. "OK," Poverman said. "Let's go."

It was simple enough. The Reverend would read statements that Poverman would repeat. After a brief preamble in which Reverend Meadly explained the beauty and importance of this glorious step toward Salvation, the ceremony began.

"Lord, I have offended thee mightily," Poverman echoed the Reverend Meadly flatly.

"Lord, I am an infection of evil that I ask you to heal and make clean," he went on.

"Lord, I ask you to break open my hard and selfish heart to allow your mercy into it that I might learn love."

"Lord, I have made the world foul with my pride."

"Lord, I am a bad man and stained with sin."

"No," Robert Poverman said out of his darkness.

"Sha," his father said. He motioned for the Reverend Meadly with his cross to go on.

"Daddy, please. Stop this. Don't." He wept.

"I am an abomination in Your eyes," the Reverend read from his paper.

"I am an abomination in Your eyes," Poverman said after him.

"*No!*" Robert Poverman shouted. Demanded. "*No!*" He stepped forward, but his father held out his hand like a rod.

"Don't be afraid," he said. "Don't you worry *now,* Sonny," he said. "I'm here." And unsheathing the great sword of his love, he waved it about his balding, sweaty head and advanced upon his Hosts in dubious battle. And fought.

Not without glory.

Old Light

Her house was her studio, a contrivance of light and space around her painting. Her work was everywhere, a dominant line. Sketchbooks, canvases, tubes, bottles, jars, frames, cans of brushes, until it all joined into its own controlling logic; but she moved about in it easily enough.

She painted anything that would hold light, but she was best known, well known, as a painter of people's faces. Not as a portraitist glorifying corporate presidents and dowager heiresses (though she had painted them all in her time), but a painter who tried to see, like her betters before her—Velázquez perhaps, Rembrandt—the soul figured forth in pigments. Her work hung in the world's great galleries and museums and private collections. And now young art historians wrote her letters and were beginning to construct treatises about her accomplishments and what they fancied was her glory.

But there was a greater glory.

"Your father slept there from the time he was twelve." She pointed through one of her large windows to a small barnlike shed. "Up top. Your grandfather and I, we slept here in the main house. And your Aunt Susan, well, we were never sure where she would turn up. With her you could never tell."

It was our delight to hear this, and our envy, I suppose. Against her indulgent but firm, creative chaos, we would compare the grumbling strictures we lived by. For our father, though an abundant man in all ways, was orderly, and as accurate as one of his T-squares.

"He gets that from your grandfather. He was orderly. But about the rest—meals and beds and clothing and where the children were—he never thought much about that, and I suppose I didn't, either. It must have put a mark upon your father."

And then, "Tell us about John Palmer," one of us would ask. Again. As always.

"Oh, you've heard all about John Palmer," she would say. "How about Winston Churchill? Or Eisenhower?"

"No, no. Tell us about John Palmer, how you met."

"I'll tell you about Rita Hayworth or William Faulkner. I met them, too. Or Enrico Fermi."

"No, no. John Palmer. You and John." And the three of us, her grandchildren, would chorus until she was borne back into that summer, into the salt-tanged days of war and love to come.

She had just graduated from art school in Philadelphia and now, in that summer, she went back to the Atlantic City boardwalk where she had in summers past drawn quick portraits in charcoal or sepia pencil or full pastels. She worked in a boardwalk store that had been hollowed out to allow room for the twelve artists, their easels and chairs, and for the crowds who became their customers to stand behind them and watch them work. A man, Joseph Brody, owned the store—the Artists Village, he called it.

There wasn't much other work to get then, and what she had really wanted to do anyway, had wanted since childhood, was to visit Europe, to see the cathedrals, the paintings, Picasso, the Left Bank, the Paris night. But now, of course, Europe was aflame. Just weeks ago we had invaded it. Even as she drew the soldiers and their girls, many had received their orders. They would all get to Europe before her, but a Europe she could not imagine now but could only fear for. Would the Cathedral at Ulm be standing? The Louvre. What would be left for her?

Atlantic City had been converted into possibly the world's largest military training base. All the hotels were made into barracks, and all day soldiers would drill on the boardwalk. But at night and on weekends, even with the special precautions taken to keep the lights from shining out to sea, the city and the boardwalk turned back to play, as if the daytime business of preparing for war was just that: a business, with regular hours and a set routine.

Everyone on the boardwalk then was from somewhere else—
Idaho, New Mexico, Maine, the west Texas hills, Louisiana, the
cornfields of Kansas. And no one was staying. Everyone was passing through, to Europe or the Pacific. Nothing was standing still.

"Time and event was in charge of all our lives, sweeping us
together and apart and yet toward a grand destiny that we all had a
share in," she would tell us. "It was—the *war* was—terrible; but
this, *this* was wonderful. A mad music. A heady wine."

About the end of July, maybe early August, in midafternoon
when the temperature had driven everyone off the boardwalk and
onto the beach, she and two other artists were taking turns mind-
ing the store. It was a Monday, slow and tired after the hurtling
weekend. Only Joseph Brody, from time to time, would whirl
through and urge them to get up and pull someone in off the
boardwalk, or maybe he even meant the beach. They paid no at-
tention. This summer she was reading her way slowly through an
anthology of American poetry. She had gotten to Whitman, and
that day, remarkably, she had just read,

> Give me the shores and wharves heavy-fringed with black ships!
> O such for me! O an intense life, full of repletion and varied!
> The life of the theatre, bar-room, huge hotel, for me!
> The saloon of the steamer! The crowded excursion for me! The
>   torchlight procession!
> The dense brigade bound for the war, with high-piled military
>   wagons following;
> People, endless, streaming, with strong voices, passions,
>   pageants . . .

when she heard a man begin to talk to her. She didn't remember
him *starting* to talk, just that he was talking when she finally
heard him.

"You're the best one, you know," he said. "I've been watching
you for two days and you are *by far* the best one. You should open
your own place, or at least you should work on your own. Is
the problem capital? There are ways around that, you know. I've
been looking around. There are three stores that would rent you
space. Here, I've got the figures." He sat down in the customer's
chair and pulled it over to her and produced a small notebook of

figures—rents, percentages, equipment, paper, mats, bags, insurance, utilities. He had it all worked out. On paper she could open her own business in a week. She was astounded.

"Who are you?" she asked. And then, "And what's it your concern anyway?"

"I'm John Palmer," he said. "Corporal Palmer for the time being. And there's no point in getting angry. You don't have to open your own business just because you could. But if you ever think about it, this is the way to do it."

Just then Joseph Brody came by and saw John Palmer sitting close to her. "What is this, afternoon tea? You. Up," he said to John. John got up and Joseph Brody pushed the customer's chair back to its proper position and then he pushed John down into it.

"Now," he said. "You want to talk, so talk." To her he said, "Draw." And then he was gone.

"Go ahead, draw," John said.

"It's OK. You don't have to. Joseph is just a little crazy."

"No. Go ahead, draw my portrait."

And so she did. As she drew he talked on and on about her possibilities, about what she could do for herself. After a time she heard that it was good talk, that there was thought and fact and imagination to it, that what he had constructed for her was, indeed, as possible as he had claimed. Finally, when she got to his mouth, she told him he would have to stop talking so she could draw it. He stopped, but she could see that it was not easy for him; though it wasn't that he was *driven* to talk, it was only that he had so much to say.

By the time she had finished, a small crowd had gathered at her back, which was what usually happened. When John got up, another person sat down.

"Here," he said, and gave her the notebook with the figures and plans.

"Thanks, it's an interesting idea but I don't want to be that permanent. I've got more to do than this. But thanks. And good luck. Goodbye."

"I'll be back," he said.

Late in the afternoon three days later he returned with a wonderfully crafted artist's easel, unique and better than any she had ever seen. It was made out of a lovely mahogany, elegantly joined, with brass fittings and buttons of a contrasting wood. It had drawers and compartments and arms that slid out of slots and turned in sockets. It even had places to hold extra canvases or boards. Most incredible of all, the whole thing could fold up as if into itself and could be carried about like a suitcase.

"For you," he said after demonstrating it.

"But where ever did you get it?" she asked.

"I made it. I designed it and I made it."

"You *made* it? But I don't understand."

"I'm a carpenter. A boatbuilder, actually, but they have me a carpenter now. I'm attached to a combat engineer unit bound for somewhere. I went to the shop and worked on this until I got it right, though I can think of ways I might change it if I ever do it again. That's the way I am."

He went to her regular easel and started to dismantle it, moving the lights, the chairs, her supplies, everything. Quickly he put the new easel—more a traveling studio—in place.

"But Corporal Palmer, how can I accept this? I don't even know you."

"It's not an engagement ring," he said over his shoulder. "It's just a piece of furniture." He turned. "And I sure can't take it with me, so you either have to take it or sell it or throw it out."

"What's going on here?" Joseph Brody descended and twirled like a tornado. "What is this?" He looked at the old easel before him and the new one in its place. He spun. He didn't know what to do. "You," he said to John, "what do you want?"

"My picture. I want her to draw my picture," he said, disarming Joseph Brody, neutralizing him.

"Oh . . . well . . . so," he turned to her, "what are you waiting for? Draw him, draw him."

And she did. Then, and again, and again, four and five or even six times almost every day or evening right through August and past Labor Day.

As in any fairy tale, the three of us bore down upon the details, waiting to savor again the familiar, excited within our expectations the way you anticipate music that you have gotten by heart.

John Palmer would come by at odd times, day but mostly night. Like many others, he was in a holding pattern, past training and now waiting for the orders to depart. Sometimes he had duties, but often not. He would come to the Artists Village and talk to her and whenever she was not busy with a customer, and when Joseph Brody would swoop down on them, he would sit and be drawn.

He would talk about *going on,* she would explain to us. It was as if he did not recognize the war, overlooked it, *refused it.* It could claim his time, but that was all. He was busy with other things that he could imagine—so busy that what he imagined became real enough to live by, as if he could actually see and touch what he was looking at through the mind's eye. And, oh, he looked at everything.

He was a boatbuilder born and reared in Warren, Rhode Island. But more than a boatbuilder. He was a master shipwright, the youngest ever in Rhode Island. He was a naval architect without the title or the schooling. He had taught himself their math and had read all their books, and then he added to that what he knew in his fingers and with it all built better boats. He told her about his triumphs, about the racing victories of Palmer boats through Narragansett Bay and beyond. Clear over to Martha's Vineyard.

He designed and invented and built boats to any task—for racing or fishing or hauling or just to row in. He was twenty-five years old but already had his own yard "stuffed with boats," as he put it, waiting for his return. But there was no arrogance to him, not a touch of it. It was confidence, rather, the self-assurance of a superb craftsman. To be so good at something that it could speak loudly enough for you, first you must be absorbed by it, taken over and humbled by it. Finally, there had to be no room for *you* in your work. She knew what he meant. They talked about the discipline and intricacies of their respective crafts, though John did more talking than she.

And then, casually, he began to wait for her until she finished working, sometimes until one in the morning or even two on the weekends, when he would walk her home, to the boarding house on a side street far from the boardwalk. But just as often they would stay on the boardwalk and walk its length, talking about the things they had done with paint and wood and about the things they were going to do, the astonishing paintings, the magnificent boats. They did not talk about themselves, or about each other. But who they were came clear, each to each, as they talked about their love of light and of straight-grained wood.

She had one day free each week, and they would go off. John was marvelous. He could produce anything. A car to take them away, a boat when they wanted, and just the right boat. He would rig a sail out of what he could find and they would poke about the sandbar islands and into the small inlets for crabs to eat late at night on a beach somewhere. Or he would sail them out to sea on a boat like a slab of wood with a sail not much more than a bed-sheet, but he would tighten everything down and make the boat do just what he told it. She never worried then. She would have sailed around the world in such a tiny boat with John Palmer at the tiller.

Those were filling days, the sea and the light bursting together, John Palmer sitting back with the mainsheet clenched in his toes like another hand, at ease in any swell. She watched him, lean and effective, to remember and sketch later.

Sometimes a Coast Guard cutter would steam up close to them as if to board them for an inspection, but they were never stopped or questioned. The cutter would steam away, men along the rail looking at them, *glad* for them, for they were charmed.

They would fish and swim and walk through the starved sand grasses and the ground-up shells. Sometimes they would walk across the sand stained with oil from a torpedoed boat, oil that may have floated across from Portugal or hung in the sea for years before coming down finally on the beach.

And John Palmer could find anything. The moon snail alive creeping across the sand, the ripest beach plums, ghost crabs. Sometimes they would go down to Cape May, to the very point of New Jersey, and watch the birds of all sorts. John Palmer would know them all. The birds and the stars and the trees and the curve and shape of everything and how it would weigh out in water or air, how it would balance.

"Gaiety," she would say to us. "It is a word I think of when I think of then."

Sometimes they would walk before the huge hotels, grey and ornate as sandcastles, with the thousands of men in them sleeping, waiting to cross the dark sea just a hundred yards away. They would walk in the salty night, carving the air excitedly into glowing images and animate shapes so sharp and firm that she always remembered them, even as the Coast Guardsmen with dogs patrolled the beaches at the water's edge against enemies, and airplanes from the mainland droned overhead looking out.

"Oh my, oh my," she would say, "but we were affirming flames."

Once they walked right into the dawn. They were not allowed to be on the boardwalk after a certain hour, but by now the patrols knew them well enough and let them be. And that night they never turned back. They clambered out to the end of a rocky jetty and watched the sea slowly brighten into day.

It was the first time John Palmer was entirely silent. They just sat there in the darkness, listening to the sea well up and hiss through the dried seaweed. They sat quietly, thinking their own thoughts but each other's thoughts, too. When he finally did speak again he said, "Maybe after the war I'll come back here."

It was the first time he had ever mentioned the war. "Maybe I'll come back and build boats. There are special problems to water like this, different from the Bay." He explained the problems. "And there are advantages." The easy cedar he could get, the oak, the wider-ranging markets of the Delaware and the Chesapeake. As ever, he had worked it all out first, not as a daydream but as a plan as exact as the boats he would design, even if he might never build them. John Palmer went about his life doing things one way.

"But what about your yard in Warren?"

"Oh, I could sell it off easily enough. A yard's not worth much more than the man who runs it."

"But you would be starting all over again."

"I don't see it as starting over, just as continuing in another place."

She thought he was going to say more, and she thought she knew what more he was going to say, but he had not thought her out fully enough to figure her into his calculations yet. Not yet, though she was sure he was working on it. The time would come. Then what would she do?

But the war came first, swiftly. Orders. Packing up. No time for a gentle leaving. John Palmer came up to the boardwalk at a busy time. It was the Sunday of the Miss America Pageant week, and she had customers waiting in line. He took his place. She did not see him until he sat down before her. He told her he was leaving in a few hours. He talked on as if the audience at her back was not there. He had found a sawmill on the mainland that had stacks and stacks of perfectly dried planks waiting. He had made an informal contract with the operator. He went on as if the orders in his pocket and the ordering of his life were not in contention. He was, as always, *going on.*

But she could not put it all together as well as he, not nearly as well. The blue September day, Miss America in the air, the density of people everywhere, the rivulets of perspiration that ran down her charcoal-smudged face, Joseph Brody flying about like a trapped pigeon, John Palmer calmly figuring the length of his dry-dock runway against the average of the tides. And the battle lines in France, defined in the maps that the newspapers were now printing each day. She could not hold it together in a pattern.

Then John Palmer was gone. She had not even time for a proper goodbye. Before he left he gave her a portfolio of all the drawings she had done of him over the summer. And he would write. Make plans. Yes. But where? Where would she be?

But he was gone. Someone else, another soldier, was sitting in his place. She drew him and how many others she could not tell. She saw nothing more. Not even John Palmer. Only a blankness.

Only much later that night, at the bone-weary end of work, did it all come together. She fell and kept falling, into autumn and into her life alone. The war had come suddenly true; the fire that was John Palmer, that had burned the mist of the war away, was banked down now. And she grew cold.

She went back to Philadelphia and set up a studio and spent days doing nothing, hearing the radio, walking about, sitting in Rittenhouse Square for hours until it became too cold, sometimes doing freelance work that a friend would call about. Her money was running low, but she was listless, a bobbing cork. There were parties, and young men who were interested in her, and professors whose pet she had been who were anxious that she begin her promising career. But she could not take hold.

She grew cold with waiting, for what she did not know. Only sometimes the thought of John Palmer would warm her, his exuberance and confidence and energy would radiate through her, and for an hour or two or a morning she would start up, mix paint, spring at a canvas, paint at what she had talked to him about in the long summer nights and on the beaches and at sea. Then she would take courage, make plans. But the winter wore on, bore her down in the snow and the shortness of things so that even John Palmer grew vague and thin and fleeting.

The war bore down on her, too, as the terrible cost of moving the battle lines in the newspaper came clearer. By February she was as vacant as February can be, as toneless as a raw umber wash on an unprimed canvas.

What was worse, she could not say what had happened to her. She was not suffering, exactly. She was not depressed or worried, only empty, as if a plug had been pulled and she had drained out.

In late March a friend showed up at her dreary studio with a letter from Joseph Brody. The friend had worked for Brody, too, and he had sent the letter this way because he did not know how to reach her. She had given him no address, for she had no thought of returning to his Artists Village or to her indentured status. His letter thought otherwise. It was the same letter she had been receiving since her senior year in high school, a letter of instructions, work schedules, arrangement of pay. She dropped it on the table. But in his envelope there were other letters to her, six of them, from John Palmer. She opened them and arranged them in order, smoothing out the thin blue paper, and she read them, long letters, and thorough.

In the midst of war there was no war, only the intimacy of personal effort and the sweep of his imagination doing this to some building or that to some machine. The boatyard somewhere along the south Jersey coast grew more tangible in his letters even than in his talk. There were sketches, bills of particulars, lists. He even asked her to send for information from certain manufacturers whose names he included.

But he saw Europe, too, and reported to her that Chartres was intact, the Louvre undamaged though all the art was hidden away, the Cathedral at Ulm still standing. He had remembered everything, every detail that she had told him about her European dreams. As best he could, he had gone about seeing Europe for her. And he saw it clearly, not only the splintered streets, rubble strewn and broken, but also the spirit and hope and achievement of civilization. She knew enough about the destruction from the daily news. It took a John Palmer in the midst of it all to remember that there was more, and that time would come, and maybe men like him, to make life whole again.

She read all the letters, then read them three times again. And she stirred like life itself in March begins to stir. Who was John Palmer? She would see.

She found the portfolio of portraits she had drawn through the summer. She had stored them in the miraculous easel. Like his letters, she arranged the portraits in an order. There were 174 of them. Through that long March afternoon she watched herself as she came to know this man almost as if for the first time. She discovered herself, too, how she had a great magic: she could find a person's humor in a charcoal line, his wit and compassion and strength and courage and fear. Through that summer she had been discovering John Palmer layer by layer. Discovering herself, too. Though she had found neither of them until now. But now she knew what she was supposed to do.

In the easel in which she had stored the portfolio there were other things—her hodgepodge of art supplies, broken shells and pieces of beach glass, sketchbooks. Opening the easel was like opening the summer again; there was even sand. And there was the anthology of poetry she had been reading when John Palmer began to speak to her. The page was marked still, the poem at which she had stopped as he began to speak.

Give me the shores and wharves heavy-fringed with black ships!
O such for me!

She had fallen in love. Now what was she to do? Could she write to the APO address on his letters? The last letter was dated in January; she had answered none. What could he have thought? Did he imagine she worked at the Artists Village all year long? She had told him that she would go back to Philadelphia, but she had had no address to give him then. Would he understand that she was not receiving his letters even as he dutifully went on writing them? But she decided that John Palmer would figure out whatever was necessary if anyone could, and that what he was doing was *going on*. The important figuring out was for her. What was she to do? And where begin?

She would write, of course, but she would go back to where she had stepped off into nothing. She would go back to where she had gotten off any path. Of course, she was going back to wait. With the kind of faith that comes to us once only, when we are young enough to believe *completely* in anything we want, she went back to Joseph Brody's Artists Village. She *knew* that someday John Palmer would come back there to do what he had said, and that he would come back for her, too. They would walk off down the boardwalk again, as if time had not happened, as if the bridges on the Rhine had not happened. He would come back and they would pick up their proper lives.

But he did not. The war claimed him after all. And her story would end.

In other years we would ask clamoring children's questions like after a tale by the Brothers Grimm, intense with the literal necessities of where and when and what and why, until the excitement of the story wore down and we were beckoned away by other pleasures.

But we were older now. *I* was.

"That's a sad story, Grandma," I said.

"Yes," she said. She had gone to the great window above the sea and watched the snake-necked cormorants resting on the exposed reefs. "Yes, it is. Sad. But it is a lovely story, too. I've remembered, you see. And proudly. Proudly."

I came to her by the window. My sisters had gone off. There was more to the story, this part of it now, as if she had waited until I had turned, was turning, into life myself. She had waited for me to allow her to come closer.

"He was a special man, John Palmer. A gorgeous human," she said. Then, "We all need—*must have*—someone like that, or else nothing will ever make enough sense. Do you understand?" She turned to me, hard and nearly vehement; but she was imploring, rather, and not angry, granting a trust now made good. "I love him still. I won't put that aside. I would not willingly lose him or give him up. Not in all these years. There's room in my life for him and for your grandfather and for all of this." She waved her hand around her kingdom in and out of the house. "John Palmer made it large enough for that. I've had all the luck."

The Editor of *A*

> . . . and whatsoever Adam called every living creature, that was
> the name thereof.
>
> Genesis 2:19

But that the view was from the twenty-ninth floor of the Kremer
Building, this might have been the office of a philologist, a lin-
guist, an old grammarian in an ancient and grand university where
the rooms, in fact or musty legend, were named for distinguished
(if forgotten) dead, where the walls were half-wainscoted in dark,
time-stained oak, where amber sherry stood ready in cut-glass
decanters upon convenient sideboards waiting for the scholars of
Trinity at Cambridge, say, to take their gentle ease from their
sweet, exquisite labors.

From the windows he could look out upon the anachronism of
Weehawken and Hoboken and to the heavily freighted ships being
tugged slowly into their greasy berths. Opposite that view, tightly
stuffed shelves of books, learned journals, facsimile copies of
manuscripts and incunabula, and string-tied bundles of unbound
proof sheets tiered up to the high ceiling; and then books and journals and sheets sloughed off like rocks breaking off a mountain,
into fan-shaped talus slopes onto the floor. But it was workable
clutter. Symington could find, with reasonable effort in the scree
of words, the exact mound and its source in the shelves. For recent
work on Urdu reconstructions, perhaps, or for the most immediately relevant disputes about the advisability of using the schwa in
describing the dialects of Indo-European languages.

Like a ballast to it all, to the wall, the office, his life, the ranks of the important and lesser dictionaries stood firm and stalwart, irrefutable, the fundamental magma; all of the Websters from Noah to the Third International, the Century's superb volumes, the four great books of the *Dictionary of American English.* Littré's venerable *Dictionnaire de la Langue Française,* the *Thesaurus Linguae Latinae.* Greek, Italian, Middle English. More. And, like majesty itself, Murray's *Oxford English Dictionary,* all its sublime volumes and supplements. Near to this, the *curiosa:* John Bullokar's start, Cockeram's earnest efforts. Fenning, Coles. Dr. Samuel Johnson's still worthy and splendid arrogances in their two original folio volumes, their leather bindings powdery. Others.

And Minsheu. *Ductor in Linguas* or *Guide into the Tongues.*

Among Symington's favorites, certainly John Minsheu stood first, this rogue, this buccaneer, this impecunious, improvident, brave and flaring genius. Himself a maker of dictionaries, more exactly an etymologist, a patient archaeologist of derivations and meanings, Symington could relish Minsheu's astonishing accomplishment, his dauntless enthusiasm, his adventurousness. Particularly that.

Symington had had no comparable adventures. He had not traveled through plague-y and bandit-ridden Europe on a lame mule to Paris, Heidelberg, Bologna, Rheims to search out the merest particle and twist of utterance. Symington had not gone hungry for his craft and subtle art, had not fled printers and their legal judgments in desperate poverty, had not debated Shakespeare and Jonson and Donne to their faces. Symington had not instructed the fabricators of the King's Bible.

Minsheu's work was first published in 1617, a full-blown attempt at an explanatory and etymological study of English with meanings in ten other languages. Ten. By fits and starts, egregiously wrong, brilliantly right. Of all the works of this kind from the past, *Ductor in Linguas* alone was still importantly consulted in the present. In his brief prefatory remarks Minsheu acknowledged "greate debtes, impossible for me ever to pay." He meant the pounds, shillings, pence that he had somehow stolen, lied, and cheated for through his determined years. But Symington had thought that Minsheu's "debtes" were now paid many times over by those who had labored after him—like Sam Johnson, who also missed meals for the price of foolscap, and Noah Webster, who mortgaged his house to meet his costs. Or Clendon, who watched the bailiff cart away the volumes of his life's work to make up accounts.

Symington thought of Minsheu now, as he looked out across the river at a ship being bent in out of the channel. The small attending tugs butted and charged at the ship like terriers herding a great cow into its manger. He had returned from his talk with Ferguson, and now he was looking out at the familiar scene and thinking of how Minsheu must have lived his life on a constant edge of adversity and disappointment, an edge so thin that no step could be calculated safely enough. Only the courage to move at all—and quickly—could sustain him, if anything could. Simply the going on. Symington held onto the thought. That was important to him. Exceedingly.

The ship slipped out of the grasp of the tugboats, the bow swinging slowly away from the wharves and back into the river. Perhaps the tug bearing against the bow had lost power, or the river, which was tidal, had unexpectedly surged as the outward-running tide quickened. The ship swung and bore down sideways toward the next wharf. Another freighter, tied up and vulnerable, was unloading there. The loose freighter would crash against it, or else trap the tug between and crush it.

Symington watched. He thought of the cargo. What had cast these vessels, these men, into this danger? Bananas from Honduras? Nickel from Mozambique? Pernambuco wood from Brazil? He thought how, out of materials, the imagination is bred to find a form in action.

The second tug raced around beneath the stern of the drifting freighter and rushed at it, its own stern churning down deeply into the river as its bow rose up against the freighter. Still the heavy drift continued, but more slowly. Then the three ships held, not a hundred feet from the moored freighter, balanced against the river and their own displacement. At last the ship was inched incrementally back and up to its proper dock and secured. Quickly the tugs moved off after another ship waiting in the roads.

There, Symington thought, was the difference between an act in time and out of time, the difference between events and remnants, the difference between Minsheu and himself. He turned from the drama at the window as from a proscenium stage, as if away from illusion. All illusion henceforth. And yet back to what reality?

If there could be anger, at least, a cleansing draught of fury and not this simple aridity like an aftertaste. But there was not. Nothing. Only Ferguson's words and the memory of the falling, the plummeting. The terrific wind and the idea of the terror.

Ferguson had told him first that the company had decided at last to begin the work it had debated for two full years, perhaps not unreasonably for such a venture, the making of a dictionary to stand in the history of the language itself. Such a dictionary would invite—demand—intense scrutiny and inevitable comparisons; thus the prestige of the company would be put at stake, ventured to some degree. Until now the company had concentrated upon the lucrative market for college dictionaries and the ubiquitous desk-type volumes, often paperbacks nowadays. In that area it had grown dominant and rich by its competence and the efforts of an efficient sales force.

But the company had always been uncomfortable that it could not presume upon some mighty lexicographic base. It did not matter, of course; the work on the college dictionaries was as exact and thorough, as respected, as any other work the staff might now be expected to do. Still, that proud factor was an important element in the two-year-long deliberations. The risk to the company's reputation (and perhaps thereby to its sales) was deemed worthy, the triumph of creating a great dictionary the sweeter for the chance. That sort of thing.

The second thing Ferguson told him was that he, Ferguson, would be the most senior editor. Symington would not be a senior editor at all. Nor the chief etymologist. He would be the editor of a letter, the letter *A*.

He and Ferguson had met at the University of Chicago in graduate school. They had gotten there just too late to have studied

with the immortal Craigie himself, or to have worked directly on
the *Dictionary of American English,* which had been compiled at
the university, but they had come close enough to the sun and its
system of disciples to have fallen into the orbit. They graduated as
scholarly linguists, journeymen if not yet fully masters of the ar-
cane, just as linguistics was becoming academically fashionable.
They might have expected jobs and futures in that direction, but it
was toward dictionaries that they had been forever turned.

Ferguson got there first, immediately, a job at once in publish-
ing, while Symington went off to teach for a time and to spend a
post-doctoral eighteen months in England, in the British Museum
and at Oxford, sifting through the tailings of the mother lode out
of which Murray's dictionary had come. Then Ferguson had called
him, put him in his place, and set him in his motion, which he
had maintained from then to now. They had stayed good friends,
intensely friends, the way people stay sealed forever when the
first weld is quickly made in the early heat of mutual discoveries
of trust.

It had always been this way. Ferguson would always tell the
truth. Immediately. So when Symington asked him why, as chief
etymologist of the company, he would not now be made either a
senior editor or the chief etymologist of the great lexicon, he knew
that Ferguson would tell him—and that Ferguson would be right,
as he had always been right about his, Symington's, career. Right
the way a good trainer or manager can be better aware than his
subject, can have a perspective that the subject cannot. And Ferguson did have that, did understand lexicography—*dictionaries*—
as he did not. All that Symington knew was etymologies. This is
what Ferguson told him, which was, of course, what he did know
about himself but had never bothered to know until he was told.
As now. And etymologies were not enough.

"The senior editors and the chiefs of sections don't even get
near words on a project this size. Not these days. They organize;
they administer. They write cajoling letters to contributing editors.
They defend their budgets to the comptroller. They make excuses
for falling behind schedule. They kick ass. Yes, and they commu-
nicate with computers. They have conferences with programmers

who don't even speak English. It's like being in New Guinea, for all that. You speak Fortran or Basic or Snowball Three. Imagine that, Sy, someday constructing the etymology of Snowball Three."

"I'm not ignorant of the process, you know. I've been here for over thirty years, you'll remember. I have, you know, worked on dictionaries recently. Successfully." But Symington was not good at the tone he wanted here.

"No," Ferguson said. "No, Jimmy, you're not, really. You've made etymologies. But that's all, really."

"That's *not* all."

They both let that settle.

"Do you want to be a senior editor?" Ferguson asked. "Do you want to be the chief etymologist?"

It was not a question but an offer. If Symington said yes, then Ferguson would do it. They looked at each other across their years and met in Ferguson's accurate assessment.

Ferguson said, carefully, "Look. All that's happening is that you're not getting what you never wanted."

It was a marvelous statement. Symington nodded. To move into a major editorship now would be a mistake. He would be unhappy, soon cut off from his research. Unmoored. Adrift.

Indeed, no such things had ever mattered to him. He had never had ambitions larger than those his work had provided for him, the ever-fining rearticulation of old languages, the digging up and delicate piecing together of verbal shards into vessels of languages increasingly remote, languages about which few cared and upon which little of importance depended. He was like an astronomer studying the light of stars that had disintegrated in eons past.

Symington's ambition had been to do his work excellently; to him, his work was like the solving of small aesthetic problems. For all the hurrahing at the professional conferences about the importance of etymological achievements to psychology, philosophy, and communications theory, Symington could not make such connections. He saw himself closer, rather, to the abstract mathematician working out the permutations of a personally invented configuration, closer to the chess scholar examining Alekhine vs. Capablanca, Cuba, 1931, closer to the composer developing the harmonic gradients of an inverted theme. It had all been as limited and as satisfying as that. For language made itself, Symington had come to believe after thirty years, and its past, like any past, did not matter at all. The past was airy thinness; only the present was flesh.

But Ferguson's announcement had broken something open, cracked a pane in the crystal dome of his life, and he had fallen through as in an accident. Sitting across from Ferguson's thin-legged table-desk, he had tumbled and clawed at the cold, dark air streaming by. He must stop this, this plunge into terror. Terror? He could not understand what was happening, could not believe his feelings even as he believed them terribly, believed in the cold wind blowing by and through him. He shook.

"What is it?" Ferguson said.

"I don't know." The shaking increased. The wind blew more fiercely, swirling now, and roaring, a roaring that filled his head until it felt swollen to bursting. The terror pulsed through him in spasms as accurate and high as waves in a precise storm.

"Sy? Jimmy? What is it?" Ferguson reached across his desk and took his hand. "Sy?"

"I don't know," he said. "I . . . don't know." Then he said, desperate to find a handhold, a ledge, or a bearing in the tumult at least, "*S*. Let me do *S*. *S* instead of *A*. Let me do the greatest letter." He said *greatest,* not *largest;* he would remember that later.

But that embarrassed them both. Ferguson let go of his hand and sat back.

"*A* is enough to do," he said.

Excellent, Symington thought. Yes. *Enough* to do. Yes. Ferguson was as loyal to language as he was to him. Ferguson would not condescend to either. Good. Symington nodded; the falling had stopped, the wind, the terror, the roaring. Only the cold stayed, and the taste in his mouth, like dry wood.

"Yes. *A*," he said.

"The editor of *A*," Ferguson said.

And now, here where he had ever been, between his blocky rampart of words and his window over the river, he must contend with what had happened, must understand what had swept over

him. For what has happened once is forever possible, and he must
know if he had fallen through his life forever. Had what happened
been simply the result of an adrenal shock, an overreaction, a disappointment that looked at first like a failure and thus a threat
against which his body had defended? It was a plausible enough
explanation, but Symington disdained it. If he stepped back from
illusion, it would have to be to a reality greater than the reductions
of enzymes and hormones racing in the blood, for mind, he never
doubted, was not simply synaptic patterns in the brain.

Then what was it?

He scanned the dominion of his knowledge and grew supple in
his endeavor, warmed and loosened by it. Reality. He considered
expertly; the cold was gone. He did not expect to find any more
than men had ever meant by it. Reality enough. But it was a vast
word, and he examined its evidences closely. 8. *Philos.* a, he concluded: *something that exists independently of ideas concerning it.*

Yes. That was his condition. 8. *Philos.* a.

The indictment was sharp and ironic and yet satisfying. He
would have to live with that. But there would be no more terror,
no painful spasms of cold fear and confusion. He would be done
with that at least. Through the small rent in his life, the momen-
tary rip, he had touched briefly the Logos, the mystery, the whirlwind. He had touched it only slightly, but enough to have felt it
tear at his mind, enough to know of the fathomless passion that he
had escaped or missed or maybe even lost carelessly decades before, or more likely never had any claim to at all—this cosmic
blare in which men lived that Adam had been called upon to
name. And Johnson and Webster and Murray and even Cockeram.

And the divine Minsheu.

But not himself.

Falling Free

Higgins looked out across the fifty yards of flat broken red caliche to the barricaded square where the men sat along the top rail. Dust spumes like sea foam rose up out of the pen into a low thickening cloud that blurred the disc of the sun in a red gauzy light. Sometimes sound, too, rose up like a yip or small hoarse cry when the men were excited. Beyond, the east side, cars and pickups were parked at random. Nothing could approach the enclosure from any compass point without raising dust. Higgins would see the contrail of dust, and the man driving would know that. He would stop his truck and get out and find Higgins to pay his five dollars and five dollars more for any passenger. Then he would go to a place on the top rail. First he might buy a can of cold beer from Miranda selling out of the trailer near the makeshift corral.

Next to where Higgins stood a brahma bull kicked against the side of the transport van. The bull did not smell the blooded dust, or else it had come to tiredness at last, worn away by old urgencies, worn away by its life. It had not serviced a cow in a year. None of the eight bulls that Higgins had brought together had. They had dried up or been injured or grown old. Tired. The bull kicked the side of the truck as if it were measuring out and counting off what was left for it to endure.

Higgins had bought each bull for two hundred dollars. He was renting the corral. His profit was not in the bull but in the twenty minutes between the bull and meat, between fury and dog food.

His profit was in the men who had come to sit on the rails and watch the bullfight for five dollars apiece.

There were about a hundred men now, but he had hoped for twice that number at least. Two bulls were dead. By now no other men would come. From the five hundred dollars he had collected, two hundred would go to the man fighting the bulls and another hundred to the ranch owner for the field and the corral. And a hundred for a couple of helpers and other expenses. He would clear a hundred dollars. Plus the beer money.

He had thought to do better. Once he had imagined bleachers full of people, not a thin line of dusty blue men perched like birds on the top rail. He had imagined a food concession and music out of a loudspeaker, horses, and bulls steaming and thunderous. Laughter. Cheering. And money enough. He had imagined it all and fed on that.

Then distantly came another tempo, rapid, clattering, rising until the air was broken into slivers and panes by the helicopters' *whack-whack-whack,* the window of the air chopped and shattered. The helicopters bore down, drilled their own wind and noise into the now-blinded scene. Higgins watched. On the side of each machine he saw through the whirlwind the large white star of the Texas Rangers.

When the motors growled off and the rotors stopped turning, the helicopters opened. The first man out was Captain Hoagland. Even from where he stood next to the transport van, Higgins could tell it was Hoagland, the size, the shape, the hitch in his walk. The captain saw him and came quickly his way.

"Higgins," he shouted when he was almost to him. "Jesus Christ, Higgins. I just can't believe you. I just can't believe you! Jesus Christ, Higgins, what in hell do you think you're doing now?"

"It's a bullfight, Captain Hoagland."

"I know that, Higgins. I can see that. It is also *Texas,* Higgins, so it can't be a bullfight. We don't have bullfights in Texas. So all this can be is a *felony* with a few misdemeanors thrown in. Now isn't that right?" The captain was on top of him now.

"There's the law," Higgins said, "and there's what the law means."

"Don't give me that, Higgins, just don't give me any of that shit. *Do you hear?*" Captain Hoagland was shouting. Two sergeants had come up behind him. Further away officers had blocked any movement from the area.

"*Do you hear?*" he shouted even louder. "*Goddamn it, Higgins, do you hear?*"

"Yes," Higgins said.

"This isn't Galveston again, Higgins. Not by a damn long shot. There is no room here for interpretation, so don't even *think* about the *meaning* of the law. Not this time, or so help me, Higgins, I'll break your ass *but good.*" And then the captain was not angry at all. He waved off the sergeants and put his arm across Higgins's shoulder and walked him away, westward, against the slight breeze that kept the whirlwind behind them, up a small rise. They looked out across to the yellow mountains.

"Higgins," the captain said, "this is cut and dried. I had it spotted from the start. I worked out the whole case beforehand. I mean, Higgins, right now the file on this case is already complete; the report is already written. It's typed with blank space left for details like the time, number of arrests, all that. I've got the law right and *tight* on this. This isn't Galveston." Then the captain laughed. "Jesus, Higgins, I swear. How do you dream up these things? Bullfighting. Jesus. Your casino or whatever it was in Galveston. And what was that thing in Lubbock? Your *employment agency* for wetbacks? How do you come up with it all?"

"That's what I do," Higgins said. "Come up with things. That's my business. And the employment agency was legal. The workers weren't legal but the agency was. We won in court."

"But bullfights are *not* legal, Higgins, now are they. Not even a little. No. You've got no room *at all* on this one. Not even a sixteenth of an inch." The captain squeezed the air to show Higgins how little was his space. "So that's what *I* come up with, Higgins. That's my business."

The two men stopped walking and the captain took his arm away from Higgins. They were silent and looked out across to the mountains.

The captain said: "You can't afford a lawyer on this one. You're broke."

"I'm not broke," Higgins said.

"Close enough," Captain Hoagland said. "Close enough." Then "How's Miranda?"

"So-so," Higgins answered. "Good days and bad. She keeps up with the medicine and it's OK."

Then they were silent for a long time. Behind them the sergeants waiting, the officers, the machines, the spectators, the bullfighters, the bulls, and the men with the winch and truck from the slaughterhouse. It might have been one more of a thousand such scenes in a common history, men waiting for their captains, who from the highland took survey of the westward world.

Frank Higgins grew up in Boston, in north Dorchester on Legion Street, which ran like a crack between the coal-shuttle poverty that rose in a tide northward through Roxbury, and the emerging gasmantel respectability of Savin Hill and Fields Corner and, beyond the Neponset, Milton. He grew up on an edge, a verge. He could cross Legion Street and walk across time, go into the roiled atavistic Irish heart crashing and bellowing out of Friday nights. Or he could go, as he would with his mother on Sundays, into the higher church of Saint Peter's on Newel Square. Ten long blocks away along Talbot Avenue with no streetcars. But in Saint Peter's on Newel Square the women wore genuine lace and the men wore vests and low-cut shoes, not high-buttoned boots. He grew up on Legion Street and never learned about boundaries, only about peripheries, horizons.

Legion Street, his home, his life there, was like a point through which an infinite number of other lines would pass. It had no dimension or extension of its own. It was like a membrane through which passed the energies of aspiration or of decline and defeat, an osmotic flow of life from one river bank to another, through a year or on any day. His father, who died when Higgins was ten, worked at what he could, back and forth, sometimes packing and icing fish until he was striped and gray as the mackerel and cod, sometimes cutting grass and raking leaves beyond Saint Peter's where there were lawns and trees. His mother boiled laundry on the other side of Boston.

He was drafted into the army in 1944, and after basic training he volunteered for Airborne. He was assigned to the 82nd Airborne Division at Fort Benning. He was a good soldier, tough, strong, obedient, resilient. And he was a good parachutist. He could land more easily than others, soften his impact and roll. Not all jumpers had his touch. In sixty-seven jumps he never turned an ankle or jammed a knee or even bruised himself. When his group had completed its training and was being readied for transport to Europe to join the division, which was already embattled at the Remagen bridgehead, he was asked to be part of an experimental high-altitude jump team.

The first time he saw Texas was when he stepped out of a C-47 at 25,000 feet. They had flown up out of a secret research station in New Mexico, but wind and weather shifts had determined them to a secondary target in the farthest reaches of Fort Bliss Military Reservation. Packed against the freezing cold, with oxygen to sustain him until he got to thicker air, loaded with telemetered instruments, he flattened his body and flew down. The chute would be opened by an automatic pressure device at 5,000 feet. That was one of the devices he was testing.

From 25,000 to 5,000 feet Frank Higgins, nineteen years old, from a Boston to which he never returned, was seized by a nearly unutterable intention to possess what from this height appeared to be the boundlessly offered. Neither then nor later could he ever explain why he felt then, just then, so suddenly certain and compelled to a destiny. It was as if he had fallen through the crack of Legion Street and had kept falling and falling until he had fallen to where he was now, above this vast continent of possibility where you could see with your own eyes that there were no ends to the earth. Falling, falling, there could be no way to go back, no means to ascend the air up and back and through to the narrow, gridded streets and rotaries of trammeled Boston.

At 5,000 feet he felt the chute release, the billowing out of it until it filled and snapped at him. Then he floated slowly down into the details of the fields and forests, the cattle and gold and silver, the rubies, diamonds, and emeralds that he could come to. The silks and spices, the frankincense and myrrh. The endeavoring.

He was sent to Europe at last, but within a month of the German surrender. After nine months of occupation duty, he was sent back to Georgia and discharged. He headed west and got off a bus in Laramie, Wyoming. In two months he was working his own sheep up into spring pastureland. Three hundred sheep. A mule with his supplies strapped to it. No dog. And a hand-scratched map to get him to the valley of government land that he was entitled to use. He lost a third of the flock to mountain lions, coyotes, wolves, steep canyons, flash-flooded arroyos, his ignorance, late snow, and the propensity of sheep to die easily. What he brought back in the fall barely paid off his loan and made him a low summer's wage, no more than if he had hired out his labor.

The captain said: "This is what you're going to do. You're going to give the money back. You don't take money for nothing. People don't pay for nothing. That's right, isn't it? So if there's no money, then there's no bullfight. No felony. You understand that, Higgins?" He didn't look at him.

"Yes."

"You give the money back; then none of this happened."

"Yes." He calculated quickly. He divided eight into five dollars. Sixty-three cents a bull. "I'll keep a dollar and a quarter for the two bulls. I'll give back three-seventy-five."

"No. No, goddamn it, no! If you keep any money, even a nickel, then you committed a crime, and I'll put you in the chopper and haul your ass to jail right now. Miranda, too, as an accessory if not worse. Now that is not only the bottom line; that is the *only* line." Hoagland turned and walked back down off the rise.

Higgins made the announcement. He stood in the center of the corral and told them, "Over by the trailer. Come over and you can get your money back. Get your money and keep moving that way." He pointed to the cars and trucks. "Don't get into line twice."

Only sixty of the men claimed their refund. To some of these he gave the cases of beer. The captain watched. Then Higgins paid off the bullfighter and the other men. The landowner he had already paid. Now he would lose a hundred or more.

Captain Hoagland came over to the trailer even as the helicopters started their engines, started to swing their giant blades and again stir the dust into a blizzard of stinging red grit.

"OK, Higgins," he said. "Now one more thing."

"There's nothing more."

"Yes, there is. There is one more thing. Get out of Texas, Higgins. Go. Soon. Real soon. Get out of Texas."

The helicopters rose, and for five minutes the air was choking and as dense as the mud- and silt-laden water of the Brazos River or of the Rio Grande near Fort Hancock or the lifeless Pecos. He had gone into the trailer and closed the door like the hatch in a submarine against the drowning of the air. In five minutes there was a hammering at the door. He opened it.

"What about the cattle?" the man said. He was one of the men from the slaughterhouse.

"Take them," Higgins said. "They're yours. They're paid for."

Before the slaughterhouse men had finished loading the bulls, all dead now, Higgins had hooked the trailer to his truck and driven off. By nightfall he had gotten as far as Balmorhea. He pulled off the road beside a small stand of cottonwood trees. After he adjusted the trailer, he carried out of the nearby stream six buckets of water that he poured into a large plastic tub outside the trailer. He stripped to the waist and washed himself, and Miranda helped. She scrubbed him hard with a washcloth, digging the dust out of all his seams, and the water in the tub turned as rusty red as blood when it falls on dry dirt.

Then they sat on two aluminum folding chairs. He drank a beer and dried and shivered in the quick cold that comes off the nighttime desert. Together they sat and looked at Balmorhea stepstoning up through the sparse growth of pinyon pine and sage as it climbed the foothills of the mountains.

"Where to now?" Miranda asked him.

Where to?

The question blossomed in his head like a sudden unremembered sound that grows louder instead of fading, as if he were approaching it, getting *to* the question more and more. The reverberations bounced back and forth, echoing. He had no orientation to it. He had never thought of *Where to,* always of *What next,* for he had lived like a caravaneer, a merchantman, a tramp freighter moving copra out of Fiji, coffee from Belém; like a Marco Polo telling himself wondrous tales in which he came at last to believe. He had always lived in the transaction rather than in accumulation itself, upon the percentage rather than the capital. He didn't know what to answer her, any more than if she had asked him where the stars come from or how life first began. She meant an ending.

"Are you thinking about settling down?"

"Yes," she said. "Time has about come for that."

"Time for that has maybe passed."

He didn't object to permanence, but he didn't know how to arrange it, what those intricacies were. He had followed opportunity like a vein of ore where every day was a surprise or a disappointment, that was all. He might have been pleased with a house, a neighborhood, a flowerbed. There had been intervals, a year near Tucson, a year in Boise, three years in Vista, north of San Diego. Pleasant enough. But there was no need in him to get somewhere finally.

He had seen that strain in many others, that restlessness like a hunger for substance. Sitting around in trailer parks, he often had heard the plans of these others to "check out" Phoenix or Flagstaff or Alamosa or Casper. Checking out a place was a disease, one of those terrible diseases when you were always hungry but all you could eat was the wind. These people went to check out the vague magic in which they were driven to believe, the luck of a jackpot, the strike. But truly they were the desperate wanderers like legend, the dispossessed for whom no place however rich would be enough to fill them, for they sought a completion, an arrangement once and for all, an end to some beginning.

Not Higgins, for whom all place was one and his. You owned what you used. He moved about in his provinces as a visitor, never unfamiliar or as a newcomer, and without expectations, though rich in hope.

But what Miranda meant was something else.

After supper, in the warm trailer, the table cleared, amidst maps, he opened the strongbox and emptied it and sorted out the papers and envelopes—deeds, receipts, bills of sale, surveys, documents of every kind, the documents of his state.

There were timber holdings in Idaho and title to the remains of a fishing camp. The loggers before him had broken the stream to the lake. They had dropped trees across the stream carelessly, impounding the lake, and it had slowly begun to die. The trees were about fifteen years away from another harvesting, and even then the smart thing would be to mill the trees right there by the lake and truck the finished lumber out, rather than transporting the logs. He had not been to this place in eight years. The buildings would be rotted out by now or burned out by hunters.

There was his gold in the Owens valley in northern California, a hard-to-work shaft mine in what was really placer country, the gold in the mine not yet leached out into the gravel of the streams. He had given the old miner a truck for the mine and a hundred dollars for his escape, and he and Miranda had worked the mine from April to early November. He had worked the gold that was there, enough for them to live for a day on what he could pound out of the rocks in a day. With big equipment, blasting, sluiceboxes, pumps, and water, he could make the gold more quickly, gain on subsistence. But he had none of these things. They moved out of the hills before the snows came to lock them in and into the winter for his planning. But by April they were in southern California on an orchard of carob trees, where they had lived for three years.

The carob trees had been fruitful, and the work was good work, open and clean and gentle after the mine shaft. They were high enough that they could look across two lower hills and see the ocean ten miles away, a small V of ocean where a chunk of land had been clipped out by an earthquake long ago. But if there was an abundance of long leather-dark carob pods full of plump beans, there was no hard market for them. He started selling cars down in Carlsbad.

He liked selling cars and was good at it. He was good at machines. He could fix the cars, not perfectly, but well enough and to varying degrees, so that when he sold the car he could match it to what the buyer needed and could pay. The young man who wanted to go fast and be shiny with a little money, the old woman who wanted the car never to break down on the freeway, the newly married, the salesman, the soldier or sailor, the divorcee with two kids. He liked selling the cars; he felt of each sale as if he had given a gift, as if the car had passed through him and become something more than an object, had absorbed some kind of blessing.

He began by working for a man, and then he started his own business, and by the end of the third year he had three lots—in Carlsbad, in Encinitas, in Capistrano Beach. Men worked for him, mechanics, a bookkeeper; telephone calls came from the large wholesale auctions in San Diego and Long Beach. He thought in two more good years, or maybe three, he could put it all together to finance a Ford or Chevy agency, used and *new* cars. He had never dealt with anything new. But the used-car business is the man, not the cars.

The last of Miranda's immediate kin, her grandfather, died. They returned to the farm in western Nebraska and lived in the house she had grown up in. For years now the farmland itself had been rented and worked by others. Nearly two sections of decent land, over a thousand acres, the barns, outbuildings, the three-generation house. Back here in Hemingford, where he had first met Miranda, the idea to reclaim this life was strong and possible. They would farm the land themselves. But in nine months a dozen distant heirs had tugged the farm apart, pulled off pieces like crows pulling at a carcass on the road.

And in nine months the used-car business was gone, and the carob orchard and the house had been rented. That was when they had bought the trailer.

It was not that Frank Higgins could not go back to anything—the carob trees, start with the cars again, complete the plan to mine the gold, cut timber, or even work at any of the numerous other jobs he had worked at in his lifetime. It was rather that some unnameable ease attracted him to every choice. No choice seemed better than another choice. Nothing had more likelihood of success for him than something else, because far larger than the earthly measurements of dollars and acreage and the poundage of carob beans per carob tree was the feeling of his hand rubbed across the texture of his life.

And this. He could not conceive of ends, as if, in the Texas sky forty years past, some of his soul, sensing the empyrean so close, had taken its own flight and left him. Having borne gravity in 20,000 feet of free fall, an acceleration that few humans can know, he lost forever a density, a weight, as if that had flown off from him the way the lesser planets lost their atmospheres eons ago. Ever after he had been unmoored, untethered by vicissitude, necessity, or even dreams.

Now he sat in the comfortable trailer to think not of an answer but of a way to answer Miranda's question. Where? What could that matter or mean? What he would do wherever he was; *that* was the point. And how could he know what that would be until he was doing it? *Where* would follow from that, as it always had.

Did she mean returning to something they owned, or might still own, or might have lost to weather or fungal spores and ice or vandals or back taxes? He held a parchmentlike paper in his hand. Once he had contracted for a crop of potatoes in Idaho, creamy, thick-skinned baking potatoes. In late September they closed all the schools in the region and the children picked the potatoes out of the furrowed wakes turned by the tractors, like gulls after grass-hoppers. For two weeks they picked his fields and all the others. Buckets into barrels, barrels into trucks. But his potatoes did not pass a rating inspection. He could not sell any of them for seed potatoes at a premium price, and so he also lost a prime rating for eaters. He sold some of the potatoes to a dehydrated mashed po-tato plant and the rest to a frozen-food processor. It was all there in his hand.

"What's left?" Miranda said.

He pushed all the paper toward her.

"I mean money. How much cash?"

He looked in a small black book. "Two thousand eight hundred and fifty-four dollars."

"Not much," she said.

"More than we've had many a time."

"I'm tired, Frank," Miranda said.

"It's been this day, this whole thing. The bullfight. It was a gamble. I knew that. I'm tired myself."

"I'm tired-er than that," Miranda said.

"That was good of Hoagland," he said.

"He's a good man," she said.

"Yes," Higgins said. "Yes, he is. Always has been. Fair. I didn't make his life any easier. I'll bet he's tired, too." He had been sorting the papers, and when he looked up Miranda was red, as red as the checks in the plastic tablecloth. She was being attacked by her blood.

He got up and helped her to their bed at the other end of the trailer.

"Take it easy now. Take it easy." He laid her down. "Where's the pills?"

"Gone," she said. "I ran out three, maybe four days ago."

"You should have told me. You should have said something."

There was nothing to do now.

"You were busy."

"I wasn't too busy for that."

"It will wait," she said. "Resting is enough."

He made her a cup of tea and sat beside her as she drank it. Then she lay back. "Well?" she said. "Have you been thinking about it?"

"What?"

"Frank, we've got to go someplace." She started to rise but he put his hand softly down on her shoulder.

"Yes. I'm thinking. I've been looking things over; you can see that." He gestured to the table strewn with places. He took her hand. It was cold, even though her face was still like the reflection of a fire.

Tomorrow they would reach El Paso by eleven o'clock and get the medicine and be on their way out of Texas by one. What was their way?

He could always find work. There was little that he couldn't do, and in the southwest and far west he knew people everywhere, and the patterns, the networks that linked up project and material and labor. They would never go hungry. In a month or two he would make his arrangements, print his business cards and stationery, establish credit, buy and sell, exchange one form of energy for another; and they would live within the synapse of things.

But now what was their way?

Miranda slept. He gathered up his realms, placed them back into the strongbox, and put it quietly under the bed.

He lowered the heat in the trailer and then stepped outside into the starry night, where it was already desert cold. Once in twenty minutes a car might speed by, the sweeping headlights dimming the stars, the sound of the car whining through the air like a heavy missile. Then the night would roll back and fill up all the spaces of darkness and silence until out beyond the trailer he could hear the scurrying of small creatures and their hunting, the taking up and giving back.

Standing in the darkness, he thought that Miranda might die. He thought he too would die. He thought that they both lived in time and that time was a place. But he could no more conceive of it, the place of death, than he could of anywhere else. He had surprised himself. Not until now had he ever thought about death, and now that he had, he couldn't make sense of it. He put his hand on the back of his neck and felt the hotness, even perspiration, his body working against the cold. Miranda was weary and ill, the run of poor luck in Texas, this sudden exodus—had that brought him to this thought? Miranda's question, was that it? *Where?* Death was *where* and life was *what?*

Deep into the desert to the east a coyote howled, and then directly away to the west another coyote answered. Above that he heard another, or was that an echo? They all howled again and yet again, and then the silence came back until he could hear the slightest but endless slurring of living and dying washing across the desert. He listened and he felt answered. He did not understand an answer, did not *now* know something more—only that he was not perplexed, not uncomfortable. He had thought about death and was surprised that he had, and he was surprised that he had not thought about death before. He decided they would go to

Vista, return to the carob farm. In the morning he would tell Miranda and that would make her easy. They would go back slowly, take a few days in Las Cruces or Tucson. Visit friends in Yuma.

And death? He came as close as he could to a decision. If death was always waiting for us all, as surely it must be, then death, wherever it was, was *someplace else.*

In the morning they rose early, and Miranda's color was nearly normal, a good sign. She could move around even though she felt heavy and slow. She would stay abed for a while more. He made them a light breakfast and set the trailer in order for moving it, turning off valves to the gas, locking drawers and cabinet doors, securing whatever might shift. Miranda would stay in the trailer, at least for another hour or two, even though it was against the law to stay in a moving trailer. Too dangerous. And in the high passes, where the road narrowed on the mountain flank into a thinness as sharp as the rim of a china cup and the downgrades punished brakes and clutch, he would bring her into the cab.

"I always liked Vista," she said. Since he had told her, she had gone on and on. "So close to the ocean as that."

"You can't see much ocean." He was drinking another cup of coffee.

"You can smell it. But that's not what's important. I know it's there, so close by; that's what's important. Growing up, that was my secretest dream, my fantasy. To go to the ocean. You know those shells? What you can hold up to your ear and hear the ocean?" She showed him with her hands.

"Yep."

"I had one of those. It was there in my grandfather's house in Hemingford when I got there. I used to hold the shell to my ear and listen to the ocean. Every day I would do that. Can you imagine? Every day. Feed chickens, goats, cows in western Nebraska and dream about oceans. Vista was as close as I got."

"I didn't know. You never told me that. We could have gotten closer. Stayed closer. We can now. Go right down to Carlsbad and get a place right near the ocean. Maybe even on the beach."

"No, Vista is fine. And I like the orchard, too. Those carob trees smell *good*."

"You never told me about the ocean." He stirred the last of the coffee.

"My secretest secret," she said.

"You never said anything."

"I've gone with you, Frank, from first to last."

"Yes, you have," he said.

"Whither thou goest, I goest," she said.

"Yes."

Though she was dressed, she leaned back on the bed, propped up on the pillow. Her hair, still long, fell loosely about her like a dappled shawl. The soft brown of it was almost all gone now into gray and white. He had asked her never to cut her hair short.

He was driving a gleaming stainless-steel milk tanker. He had come out of Wyoming into Nebraska and wintered over in a hard job in a small machine-shop in Scottsbluff, welding mostly but fabricating steel too, as well as doing a lot of auto body work. He had gotten very good at that and could draw as fine and straight a bead as anyone in the shop and then grind it off so you could never tell where the join was. He helped to make what was one of the first milk tankers in Nebraska and took the job of driving it. This was about 1948, just as the movement away from milk cans was starting. The dairy cooperatives were taking strong shape, and the milk tankers followed that naturally. He would drive out on a route and suction the milk out of the farmers' holding tanks into the steel tanker. No more rutted, rattling hauling of milk to the milk-train depot by the farmer over roads that would sometimes churn the milk in the heavy cans into butter.

By the time he reached the Keane farm where Miranda was raised by her grandparents, he would have already driven half a day's work, because he had started in the early dark morning. He would break for lunch, sit in the Keane kitchen, and eat whatever he had made for himself and drink the fresh coffee she would have ready.

In a month she was preparing him his meals. Twice a week he would back the great silver tanker up to the dairy barn and pump the milk and then come to the kitchen, where his food was waiting. She began to challenge herself to surprise him, to prepare something new and unexpected, and then they could talk about that, the food, before they got to talking about other things. She would make an apple pie laced with cinnamon and shavings of lemon peel, chicken ground up and rolled in a blanket of thin crusty dough.

By the second month she was ready to leave with him, and by the end of the third month she did. Properly enough. They were married first, right there in Grandfather Keane's house. Then she got into the tanker cab with him and drove away. Twice a week she would come back with him to the farm, but two months after their marriage they were gone, off to Wichita, where he had heard that Piper and Beech were looking hard for skilled metalworkers, aluminum instead of steel, but close enough. They would go there, whether to actually make airplanes or not. The airplane was coming, that was certain—the future was flying in with it. They should be where they might best find whatever they would come to look for. Besides, over the courting table laden with food, he had never implied to her a life like the one she had, a longitude and latitude to stake down a life upon, ten chains and six links wide, forty rods deep. Nor had he implied or promised adventure or riches or success of some special sort. Not even expectations. All he had promised was Utah and Nevada, Texas, the Rockies and the Sierras, the Colorado watershed, the western world. And all that it inherit.

She had gone with him and had worked where there was work for her to do. Was it a gypsy's life? More Indian, she thought, more like the Nez Percé following the buffalo or waiting for the returning elk, more like the tribes on the coast taking fish in the surf or the upstream salmon, more like the Shoshone moving from spring roots in Utah to October nuts in Idaho. Yes, like Indians. She liked that.

"Well, we should start. I want to get to El Paso by eleven. I'll bring you up front in an hour or two."

"Fine."

"If it gets too rough back here, call me on the intercom."

"Yes, Frank. I know."

"OK." He started out.

"Frank."

"Yes."

"I'm feeling fine. Don't worry. I'm feeling real good."

"You're a tough old woman," he said. "I'm not worried."

"And Frank. I'm really glad about Vista."

"About settling down, is what you mean."

"Yes, Frank. I suppose I do. I suppose I do."

He eased out onto Route 10 slowly, letting the wheels settle and hold, and then he applied more power much as he might with a team of horses, letting them lean into the weight. Or maybe it was the way a ship would ease away from a dockside berth into the current.

The truck pulled the old trailer easily enough. He remembered when they had bought the trailer twenty years before, a sparkling Airstream, the best, a Wally Byam special, twenty-eight feet, solid, with all the comforts. Now the trailer, still sound, was pitted and oxidized.

He enjoyed driving this rig. He thought it was good that a man who drove so much should take pleasure in it, and he sometimes considered that maybe they moved about because he needed to feel from time to time the long pull up a grade as now, dropping down a gear as the mountain started to stiffen, his power and the power of the truck merged. He knew this road. In fifty miles the mountains would flatten out, flat as a piece of slate, but only for about three hundred yards; then they would rise again for another fifty miles when the road would begin its long, twisting, eighty-mile descent to El Paso. At the flat spot he would bring Miranda up into the cab.

El Paso, Tucson, perhaps to Kingman and across the true desert and down at last to Vista. He laid it out before himself like a good captain, an old and experienced mariner, a hand steady and proud on the helm, homeward bound and a good voyage out.

Homeward bound. Frank Higgins tried to grasp that, but it slipped away. He could understand what Miranda must mean by that idea and what she wanted, and he was glad enough to give her that, to take her where she wanted to go and to stay with her—he had no other *need*—but he could not find that kind of centering in himself. He drove on, miles into tens of miles.

Between the simple counterpoint of engine and transmission and figured road song he heard the high, nearly breathless note, a harmonic almost above the range of human hearing, and he felt just then the least imbalance, the tug of the trailer the way a sea change might begin in the shifting angle or pitch of a small wave. He gave the truck more gas like a probe, but against the rising revolutions of the engine, the speed of the truck fell, the gas-vacuum ratio turned down, temperatures rose, pressures increased or faltered. He watched a trouble being announced by all the sensors. The high sound turned piercing, shrill; a vibration began like the strumming of a steel string.

In two minutes more he decided the trouble must be in the wheel bearing of the trailer on the right side. He was about eight miles from the flat spot in the mountain, and he would have to make it to there. He could not stop now. The axle could seize up or weld. And there was nowhere to stop. Between the paved road and the guard rails, where there were guard rails, there was not a trailer's width of shoulder, not half a trailer's width. But he thought he could make it to the flat spot. He had spare bearings. If the axle was sound and not bent by then, he could make the repair. He would have to chance it, but chance itself was his vehicle, had always been.

Moving as slowly as he could now to keep the heat from building on the axle, he could look out over the canyonland more than he had on faster crossings of this terrain. He had never been down into the gorges and cuts, only on this or on other roads, 67 or 85, passing above the canyons and draws like on a bridge over a canyon one would imagine to be like the canyons in hell that the preachers would scream and weep about. Maybe that was where they got the image of their hells. He drove slowly, fifteen miles an hour, and thought how he had heard preachers describe just what he could see now at the bottom of the Apache Mountains. They called it hell and threatened him, threatened them.all, with it.

In ten minutes he would know how long it would be before Miranda got medicine. If necessary he would take her in the truck

directly to El Paso and return for the trailer. He would not like
that. The trailer alone at the pullout would be game, quarry, to
any who had a mind for it this far away from anything. And this
was Texas still, the west of Texas.

He rolled the truck and trailer to a soft stop at the farthest end
of the pullout. The brakes were firm, undamaged by the heat. He
went quickly to the wheel. It was the bearing all right, the inside
bearing. It was steaming, burning off the very last of the grease
and sucking the slightest moisture out of the air, turning that to
blue steam. He would have to let it cool by itself. Miranda came
out of the trailer.

"What's wrong?"

"Can't tell yet. It'll take about a half-hour to cool enough to
pull the wheel so I can see the axle."

He looked at her closely. She seemed steady enough.

"What's up? You need help?"

From under the trailer where he had been working, Higgins
looked out at the man's booted feet. Worn army boots. And
worn-out green fatigues. He squirmed out and stood up and
looked at the man. In his late twenties. Across the bridge of his
nose was a deep fresh cut. Elsewhere he was scratched a little,
torn.

"A bearing," Higgins said. "I think I can fix it here. Fix it
enough to get going anyway."

"Is that right? That's terrific. You can really do that?"

"Maybe."

The man carried a large new backpack, an elaborate carrier
with a complication of pockets. He swung it off his shoulder to the
ground between them.

"But you'll need help. Then I could help you, right?"

Higgins said, "And?"

"And then you could give me a lift to El Paso." He rubbed his
dark, heavy hair up from his eyes.

"This will take time," Higgins said. "Maybe a lot of time. You
could do better sticking your thumb out."

"Nothing hardly moves on this road," the young man said. "And the semis, once they start moving, they don't stop for nothing, not going up, they don't. And who's in a hurry, right?"

Higgins said nothing. He turned back to the wheel. Miranda opened the trailer door and looked out.

"Hi," the man said. "I'm Joe Smith."

"Miranda Higgins," she said. "Pleased to meet you." She looked around for her husband.

"I'm going to help you fix your trailer."

"You'll have to excuse me, Mr. Smith. I'm not feeling up to snuff. I'm in here resting. Frank?" she called.

"Yes?" he said from where he was working.

"Let me know if you want anything."

"You just take it easy, Miranda Higgins," Joe Smith said. "I'll help him. You just rest."

They got the trailer jacked up enough to pull the wheel. Higgins could have managed alone. Joe Smith did not know anything about the task, but he was eager to be useful. He talked ceaselessly, offering advice, opinions, judgments about everything. To Higgins it sounded like pieces of a lot of different jigsaw puzzles: even if you could fit them somehow together, they would not combine into a picture of something recognizable.

"How did you get here?" Higgins asked.

"A guy dropped me."

"Here? Right in the middle of the mountains?"

"Right," Joe Smith said. "We stopped. I had to take a pee. The next thing, he drives off. The son of a bitch."

Higgins didn't believe him. How did he get his backpack out of the car if the guy drove off? But he didn't ask or challenge him. If Smith was lying, why? And how in fact *did* he get here, to nowhere? And without a hat? But maybe he didn't want to know that either.

"There it is," Higgins said. "Shot to hell."

Joe Smith crowded over him. "What?"

Higgins pointed out where the seal had broken and the grease had been lost, where the outer race had been cracked by the friction from the heat so that the bearings had fallen out.

"So that's how it works, huh? Great. I never knew. Now what?"

"What did you do in the army?" Higgins asked.

"I wasn't in the army. I wasn't in any service."

"Well, you sure look like you were in the army," Higgins said.

"This is like a costume. People see me this way and think I'm a Vietnam veteran. It makes things easier mostly, but let me tell you, some people get very uptight. If they think you're a veteran, they think you must of done a lot of killing of people. Not me. I was never near the army. I was a C.O."

"So why do you wear the uniform if it gets you trouble?"

"Not trouble, not exactly trouble. But it doesn't matter to me."

"I guess you must've gone to college," Higgins said. With a hammer and cold chisel he was driving the old races off the bearing block and out of the way so he could get down to the axle itself. He could see already that it was badly scored.

"College? Oh yes. Oh yes, oh yes, oh yes," Joe Smith laughed—a pleasant laughter, low and full and expanding, not the kind of laugh that went with the rest of him, with the sharp, nearly brittle chattering, the quick nervous talking. "In college and out, up and down, coast to coast, Canada to Mexico. Oh yes, I spent a long time in college. And I'm not through yet, either."

"You've got a lot to learn, is that it?" Higgins offered. But Joe Smith missed the joke.

"Do I? Oh yeah," he said. "Yeah."

Now that the shaft of the axle was clear, Higgins could see how badly scored it was. It would have to be smoothed out, filed down, or else the new inner race would be chewed up in less than a mile. He explained this to Smith.

"You want to do it?" he asked. It would be hot and slow and dirty work.

"Sure. Sure, I'd love it. Show me what to do."

"Nothing to it. Just file. Bear down going, ease up coming back. Soft strokes. The main thing is to keep moving around the shaft so you don't get a flat spot." He showed him with a few strokes.

"Slowly," Higgins said. "Take it easy or you'll take off too much metal. Easy."

Miranda came out of the trailer, which was getting too hot now. The air conditioning could only work off the car engine or an electric hookup. He set up the aluminum chairs and two umbrellas that attached to the chairs with flexible handles. They sat down and watched Joe Smith.

"I was born on the road," he told them. "I'm a traveling man. It's in the blood. My father was a salesman, but my mother actually moved around with him a lot. Not all the time, but a lot. I was born in St. Joseph, Missouri."

Miranda said, "It sounds like what you hear sometimes about old-time actors, vaudeville folk, the baby born backstage, and the trunk his crib. I read where Al Jolson was born that way, raised that way."

"Yeah," Smith said. "That's it. Raised in a trunk. Who's Al Jolson?"

"He made the first talking picture. He was a singer on the stage, you know? It was a big success, the picture. He was very famous for a while. But that was a little before my time." She smiled. "I'm not so old as I look."

"Yeah," Joe Smith said. "I bet a lot of famous people have come out of trunks." He laughed deep and wide again and turned back to the axle.

"What did your father sell?" Higgins asked.

"Whatever anyone was buying," Smith said.

"Well, I sure know something about that," Higgins answered.

"But clothing mostly. To department stores. Shopping centers. Mostly clothes. I was always well dressed. He should see me now."

"Is he still on the road?"

"Hawaii. He's in Hawaii now, retired. My mother, too."

They talked on, but with Joe Smith mostly doing the talking, setting the pace. Higgins didn't believe half of what Smith said, maybe not a third. He was like a character out of his own swift inventions. And Higgins didn't understand many of the connections Smith made, or rather his failure to make the connections. But he *was* entertaining, a pleasure to Miranda, who was resting and easy. And now there was time enough for everything. Time enough. . .

"For shoes and ships and sealing wax, and cabbages and kings," Joe Smith said, shifting, spurting away from something else he had been saying.

"What's that?" Miranda asked. "That sounds nice, whatever it is."

" 'The time has come, the walrus said,/To speak of many things,/Of shoes and ships and sealing wax/And cabbages and kings.' Alice through the looking-glass. Alice in Wonderland."

"Is that right?" Miranda said. "Fancy that."

"The axle," Higgins said. "If we're going to make it to El Paso before dark." He pointed gently.

"Right," Joe Smith said, "right," and ducked back to his work, but out again in the same motion the way a rubber ball bounces back off a wall. He dropped the file. He looked up at them as if he had found something that he must share. "*Nothing is but seeming makes it so.*" He said that with such intensity, with so tight a focusing of certainty and yet a certainty awash in some sea of grief, that none of them could move for some moments. What could be born of that? They all held like a stopped frame in a movie.

"The axle," Higgins said at last, freeing them.

"Ah," Smith breathed out, a sigh or a gasp. He returned to work and completed some part of some thought at the same time, saying he should have stayed in Costa Rica where they can grow three, even four, crops of anything in a year. Bananas, papayas, corn, sugarcane, coffee beans, Mary Jane.

"Mary Jane?" Miranda asked.

"Grass," he giggled. "Pot, weed. Marijuana."

"Lunch?" Miranda said. "Who is for lunch?"

Miranda prepared tunafish salad sandwiches and lemonade and opened a jar of small sweet gherkins. Higgins finished up trueing the axle, getting it ready for the new fitting.

"After lunch we'll put it together and see what we have."

"Maybe it won't fit," Smith said.

"Maybe."

"Then what?"

"Then I'll have to think of something else."

"Then?" Smith asked. "Not until then?"

"Right."

"Great," Smith said. "Terrific. You're my man, my main man. My way of thinking exactly. Never get to an idea before you need it." But that was not what Higgins meant. He meant that you didn't get to a knot until someone or something had pulled the strings. But *ideas* were something else. Ideas had to do with what you valued. Ideas were not objects; they were how you *saw*.

But Higgins could also understand Joe Smith's response, how he could think or feel in his piecemeal way. They were as different as day and night about that, all right, but Higgins felt that they did share this other urging. Men were the same whatever you called them; that was indisputably true. But what Smith said, *Nothing is but seeming makes it so,* could be true also. Higgins was comfortable with that, too. He understood that, and the two ideas did not seem in dispute.

They ate the sandwiches and drank lemonade. Only at long intervals would some vehicle pass on the road, usually a laden truck pulling a thick black streak of greasy diesel smoke across the colorless sky.

"So you're going to El Paso?" Higgins said. They were drinking coffee now.

"If that's where you're going, then that's where I'm going. OK?"

"Then what?"

"I do my thing, you know? I'm a photographer. I go around taking pictures of the world."

"Yes?" Higgins said. "Is that right?"

"My trouble is I don't do that much work; that's what it is. I spend a lot of time gathering things, traveling. Getting in touch with my subject. Meeting you and Miranda."

"I'm sure that's important," Miranda said.

Higgins said nothing now, but waited, certain that Joe Smith was going to tell them more, to explain. The questions had primed some pumping necessity in him. Higgins had heard men tell about themselves for forty years; unbidden, they called forth their histories like an act of certification, a demonstration of some personal and private faith that gave them the right to their existence.

"I do other things," Joe Smith said.

But his voice, the tone of it, changed. It had, in the instant, rarefied, thinned. The high-pitched crackle of his rapid speech, the fitfulness, clicked off; and now this lightness of sound, sharp, translucent. It sounded like a ghostly voice on the radio late at night coming from a far-off station, but faintly and fading. It was as if his voice had forgotten who he was.

"What kind of things?" Miranda asked. "What kind of other things? I should think you'd be busy enough taking pictures. And all your moving around. That's nearly a job in itself, isn't it, Frank?" She turned to him. "Yes, we can tell you something about that." She reached across and poured Smith some more coffee.

"I collect bugs. I went to Eugene, Oregon, to visit a friend, and I got a job there at the university collecting insects for a scientist. In the morning I'd empty the traps we set overnight and he'd show me what to do, how to sort them. I'd sort out what we got. You wouldn't believe it, how many different insects there are just in a field in Oregon."

Two helicopters flew out of the sun, one slowing for a moment above them. They flew like extraterrestrial birds of prey, glinting and banking in the sun. Occasionally one of the helicopters would drop down near the jagged, rotted canyon floor and then rise, swing up and away, raking the canyon. One came down fast and low over them and paused like a greeting and a warning, flicking at them with the tip of the rotor like a whip. The white star was clear.

"Hoagland," Higgins said. "I'll bet."

"Yes," Miranda said. "I think you're right."

"Checking up," Higgins said.

"Yes," Miranda said.

"You know them?" Joe Smith asked.

"Hoagland is a captain in the Texas Rangers," Higgins said.

"And an old friend," Miranda smiled.

"Checking up to see we're moving out." He and Miranda both laughed at that. Then he explained the rest to Smith. "We've got to leave Texas. Hoagland's making sure."

"Trouble?" Smith said.

"Of sorts. Trouble for Hoagland. You might say we're doing him a kind of favor. Him and us." He and Miranda laughed again.

Smith was attentive. His old voice returned, moved out of his head and back into his body. "I've got to hear this. You're running from the law?"

"Hardly running, I'd say," Miranda said.

"Right now we're not even moving much," Higgins said, "but maybe we'd better."

"Yeah. Sure. You're not *running* but you are *leaving*. Just as long as you keep heading *out*." Smith pointed somewhere in the direction of New Mexico. "Out and you're OK. East and you're in trouble. That's it, isn't it?"

Higgins got up and went to the trailer axle and the work to be done. Smith said: "But what were they looking for over there? If he saw you here, what was he looking for over there?" He waved across the canyon where the helicopters had flown.

"They're always looking for something," Higgins said. "Or someone. People get down in there and get lost. Sometimes I think they just like to ride around in the helicopters."

Behind them, to the south and east of them, they heard an explosion, a small burst that moved back up through the valley from the direction in which the helicopters had gone. The sound kept its shape high in the air, a small firm report that moved toward them and past like an old cannonball. Far off, nearly at the limit of what they could see, a heavy cloud of iridescent red powder sifted quickly down to the canyon floor.

"They're marking something," Higgins said.

They got the bearing back together, packing it with grease, driving the races tight. There was too much play in it to trust it far, but it was tight enough that he could nurse it to El Paso.

They drove off with Miranda sitting between the men in the cab of the truck. The air-conditioner hummed. In ten miles the trailer began to yank again, but only a small tugging. Higgins said nothing. Even at the forty-five miles an hour at which he held the rig, they would make El Paso in less than three hours. If the trailer bearing went bad again, he would leave it and drive on in the truck. Let Hoagland make of that what he would.

At the thought the helicopters came back over them, racing now toward El Paso. They were not looking for anything.

"How are we doing?" Miranda asked.

"Fine," he said. "Just fine."

Joe Smith sat quietly looking out at the canyons, his large new backpack jammed in between his legs and knees. Higgins had told him to put it in the back of the truck, but he had said no. "This is my life," he had said. "I go nowhere without this, not two feet away."

"Is that how come you got it now? The guy who left you didn't drive off with it?" Higgins had asked.

"Yeah, that's right."

"Well, we're not going to drive off without you. Not likely. And we'd all be more comfortable with that in the back." But Smith refused.

They drove along, the sun dropping over its zenith slightly now and down a little before them. The blanched sky grew whiter still.

He thought about Joe Smith, who he was, who he could be, what he was doing here. He felt no particular alarm. The man lacked menace, the furtive attitude, the hanging tangle of danger, the jut of anger in the eyes that you came to recognize on the road. Frank Higgins believed he could read it all in the way a man stood or moved on the highway shoulder, even at fifty-five miles an hour and a hundred yards away. Violence had its own posture.

But there was more to it, to him, that raised in Frank Higgins a sympathy, an old recognizable resonance beyond the saying of it. Though Joe Smith may have done all the things he said or implied, Higgins didn't believe that was the actual man or that he had a purpose with shape and angles and bulk to it. What he did or had done or *might do* was all the same to him, an undifferentiated image of going on. So whatever Joe Smith told them was not a lie even if it was not the truth.

"What about you?" Joe Smith asked. Higgins started, as if maybe he had been speaking his own thoughts aloud and Smith was asking him back some of his own questions.

"We're going to Vista, California," Miranda said, as if to forestall Higgins, prevent some vague words that he might say that would deflect them. "We've got a house there and a piece of land, some carob trees. A little of this and a little of that. Home," she ventured.

"You're going to retire?" Smith said.

"You might call it that," Miranda said.

"What are you retiring from?" Smith asked. "What do you do?"

"I'm a photographer," Higgins said.

"Oh, Frank," Miranda said.

In another mile Smith said that he thought he might get a boat and sail around the world.

"I'd start in San Francisco and I'd go to Hawaii, to see my parents, you know? Oh man. Surprise them. Then I'd just keep on going. Japan, India, Africa. Whatever came next."

"Quite a trip," Higgins said.

"Yeah. But people are doing it all the time. You read about it all the time."

"It would take some good money to do that, I'd imagine," Miranda said.

"It's not the money. Money's not important. Money's not the problem."

Two of the helicopters came back over and past them.

"That's right," Higgins said. "Money's never the problem." But he was sorry to hear Smith's voice change again, as it had before, into the thin whetted blade that he seemed to be holding against his own throat.

"What do you do?" he asked Higgins again.

Higgins recounted some of his history, preferring to hear himself rather than Joe Smith's voice. He told him of his most recent activities for which he was leaving Texas. He told him of his territories, his gold and timber and borax. He showed him some strands of the long events he and Miranda had raveled up into the robes they wore now. He even explained to him something about the *plausibility* of worth. His life was what he made it, and that way could be worth neither more nor less than what it was, nothing you could put on a conventional scale.

After a time Smith said to all of that, as though he had not listened, "You don't think I'll sail around the world, do you?"

"You can't sail a boat, can you?" Higgins said. "So how are you going to sail around the world?"

"I'll learn," Joe Smith said. He nearly shouted it, but his voice was so high and lean that what he said was nearly a breathless whisper. Then he was silent.

Frank Higgins watched the road and felt the rig vibrate, and he thought about Joe Smith and about himself. The young man had mystery in him, but it frightened him, as if he wanted answers but would despise the answers he might get, as if the more he learned the less he would be able to ask. But Higgins wasn't one to say such things to anyone. Let each take to himself what mystery he can. Still he understood Joe Smith, so even when Miranda said to him, quietly, through his reverie, "Frank, he's got a gun," he did not feel mistaken or uncertain, or even alarmed. He knew Joe Smith too well for that.

"What the hell are you doing with that?"

Smith put the gun, the hand with the gun, inside the army field jacket, as if he didn't know what he was doing with the gun. As if he was embarrassed.

"Listen," Smith said. "This is the problem. You've got to understand the problem. I don't want to go to El Paso. But this trailer is safe, see? Isn't that crazy? But not to El Paso."

"She needs medicine. Let me explain about the medicine." He told Smith quickly about the hydrochlorothizide. "She hasn't had the medicine for four days now. Five. That's why she's feeling poorly."

"That's a problem, Miranda," Smith said. "That certainly is *another* problem."

"There are no problems until you get to them," Higgins said.

"Yeah. That's right. I believe that. So . . . well, what next?" Smith giggled.

What next.

"There's no problem that I can see. There doesn't have to be a problem. If you want money, you came to the wrong trailer. If you want a ride, fine. We go to El Paso. We get the medicine. We move on. You stay with us and you have safe passage, if that's what you need. I'm not asking you why. I'm not asking you anything. You just get off wherever you want. The *problem* maybe was when you pulled the gun. You don't need that.''

''I don't even know how to shoot it,'' Joe Smith said.

''Well, it's easy enough to do. No different than a kid's toy gun. Just pull the trigger, that's all. So you be careful.''

''OK.''

They drove on. One helicopter went over them toward El Paso. Joe Smith spoke in his normal voice again.

''Yesterday afternoon I was in Guadalajara. This morning I was across the river from Juarez. Now I'm here. This guy gives me the gun and the backpack. This is in Guadalajara.'' He patted the bag between his legs. '' 'That's a million bucks of goods in there, amigo,' he says. He wasn't Mexican, but he talked that way. Amigo. 'You be real careful, muchacho. If a guy shows up in a red Thunderbird, give him the bag. You know what a Thunderbird looks like? But if somebody else, *anybody* else, shows up, start shooting, amigo, because they come to shoot *you*. You understand? Chico here is a good pilot. He'll get you in and out and back for your money. But believe me, no red Thunderbird, shoot, man, and get out. OK? OK. Chico?' How about that?'' Joe Smith said. ''How about that?'' He shook his head.

''The plane crashed?'' Higgins said.

''Yeah.''

''I don't feel too well, Frank,'' Miranda said.

''Just rest, Miranda. Just rest, dear. We'll be in El Paso in a couple of hours.''

''There's medicine in New Mexico,'' Joe Smith said.

''There's police in New Mexico too,'' Higgins said.

''No one's looking for me there,'' Smith said.

''No one's looking for you here,'' Higgins said.

''Maybe.''

''The plane crashed. What happened?''

''I don't know,'' Smith said. ''We were flying real low. Right down in the canyon, and then we smacked into rock. Chico was killed. The plane didn't burn, but Chico was good and dead, I

could tell that. I got thrown out. Crazy. Nothing happened to
me. Just this cut." He touched the bridge of his nose. "So where
am I?"

"Hell, you've got no problem," Higgins said. "You didn't
do anything. You walked away from a crash, that's all. No crime
to that."

"And this?" Smith said. "What about this?" He patted the
backpack again.

"Throw it out the window. I'll slow down so you can do it.
Throw it out the window and keep moving. So what's your problem? You got no problem. Here. I'm going to slow down. Open
the window."

"You're kidding. You've got to be kidding. You know what this
is worth? This is a million dollars. You want me to throw this
away? How can I do that?"

"Easy."

"Not for me."

"Don't be dumb. Figure it out. You can't give it back to your
friend in Guadalajara."

"No friend. *Harold,* that's all. No friend."

"You can't give it back to Harold. And you can't do anything
with it. Maybe it's worth a million to someone, but it's not worth
that to you. To you it's nothing but a bag of hay."

"Cocaine."

"A bag of dust, then."

"I'll figure it out. I'll do something with it."

"Somebody will either kill you for it, or you'll end up selling it
a little at a time like one of those small-time pushers you read
about who are always getting caught and sent to jail. I'm going to
slow down. Throw it out the window. Live."

"It's my chance," Joe Smith said. Pleaded.

"Your chance for what?" Higgins demanded. But Joe Smith
could not say, Higgins knew. He could only have said things
he could buy with the money—cars, clothes, women; maybe the
boat itself, but not the trip around the world. With that kind of
chance he could not have answered even if that is what he
would have wanted to say. There are the chances we take and

the chances that happen to all of us. Joe Smith didn't know how to tell the difference, and Frank Higgins didn't know how to tell him.

"Frank," Miranda said.

"Just rest, dear. Don't worry. We'll get medicine."

"Maybe she needs more than medicine," Smith said. "Look at her. Jesus, look how red she is. I've never seen anything like that. Maybe she needs a hospital. What then? You take Miranda into a hospital in El Paso and I sit in the trailer on the street with a million dollars worth of coke? You're kidding. They spotted the plane. You know that. You saw that. They'll be looking for me. They'll be looking for *somebody*."

Higgins thought Miranda might very well need to go to a hospital, and maybe she would have to stay. But he said, "No, no. We've been through this before. She'll get the medicine from the emergency room." If he could get into the city, as far as that.

Route 10 began to scribe a large switchback against the mountain, a turn so large that from the upper level of the road you could look down on the lower level coming back at you in the opposite direction. Right at the turn in the switchback a dirt road went down into the bottom of the canyon. For a good distance the white thread of the road stitched across the rotten stone of the valley floor. Smith took out his gun hand.

"You see that road. Pull off down that road."

"If I get this rig going down that road, I won't be able to get back up," Higgins said.

"That's right," Smith said. "We're going down. We're going across." He opened the glove compartment to rummage for maps.

"The southwest is right on top," Higgins said.

Once down into the canyon, the trailer strained and bumped along roughly. Then Smith told him to stop. He gave Higgins the map he had been looking at.

"Where are we?"

"Here," Higgins said. "Right here." He pointed out their junction. Smith studied.

"OK. Fine. See here, this road, it's not even marked? We'll just follow it right across to"—he paused to read the map—"to Carlsbad. See? New Mexico."

"That will take a day to do with the trailer, on a road like this. We'll leave the trailer. We'll go in the truck."

"No. Oh no. The trailer makes us safe. Your friend in the sky sees the trailer, sees you heading to New Mexico, he'll figure Good. Right on. No. We keep the trailer."

"And Miranda?" Higgins said to him.

"Frank," she said.

Smith told him to get out of the truck. By the side of the trailer, the shady side, they talked. The heat down in the canyon was dry and whiter than the sky. "Jesus, what have I got here?" asked Smith. "What am I going to do?"

Higgins wanted to give him an answer. Smith would not just throw down the coke and walk away—the only answer was to do what Smith was doing, keep the backpack.

"You think it's so simple," Smith said.

"No," Higgins said. "I can see your problem."

"I'm not going to throw the coke away. *I can't.* You've got to understand. If I throw the coke away, then nothing makes sense at all; then there will never be anything for me that will ever make sense. I'll be through. Finished."

"You'll always be running, hiding."

"I am now, goddamn it. *I am now.* Running, hiding, looking around. So what's the difference?"

"You *never* know that, the difference," Higgins said, passionate, certain. He half rose. "You're wrong to think that way. Listen to me. I know."

But Smith shook his head.

"I'm not going to work in some factory," he said.

"No," Higgins agreed.

"It's all so disappointing." He looked into the desert and then back at Higgins. "I thought there were so many parts to play. I was going to play them all. Now look at me. I was going to live in wonderland."

Higgins was silent.

"Everywhere I turned, it all felt used up. Completed. Signed, sealed, delivered. I used to think it was me. That I was some kind of freak. But it's not me. Not me *alone*. There's nothing left. This is what's left." He kicked the backpack.

There was nothing he could tell Smith now, nothing he could tell him to do that would make the doing easy enough, or even possible. He could have told him what he would have done at Smith's age, what he had done, except that Smith had been broken exactly by what Higgins believed: that he was a potentate, and that any rock he held in his hand was a jewel. He would have kept the cocaine, whatever else he would have done with it. Maybe buried it. But he would have kept it. But possession, of anything, would destroy Smith. At 25,000 feet Higgins had fallen free. And now for Smith it was too late.

"Hey, Higgins," he said. "Frank? How about going partners. We'll get to San Francisco. We'll get the boat. We'll both learn to sail. You, me, Miranda, around the world together. Who wants to go alone anyway, right? What do you say?"

"Sure," Higgins said.

They both sat silent now, compressed beneath the lowering heat, desert heat, until there was nothing left. Higgins got up.

"Where are you going?"

"I'm going to get Miranda out of the truck. It will be heated up in there by now. The trailer will be cooler."

"Yeah. That's right. Get her out of there."

Higgins walked to the truck. He eased Miranda out and carried her to the trailer, and inside he laid her gently on the bed. The air in the trailer was close but far cooler than in the truck or outside.

"I'm so dizzy, Frank. I'm so worried."

"Now don't worry, Miranda. Do you hear? We'll be out of here soon enough. This will be ended. Close your eyes now. Just close your eyes."

"Be careful, Frank."

"Close your eyes, Miranda. Sleep."

He waited until she closed her eyes and waited until he was sure she would relax enough to keep them closed.

"Rest," he said. "Sleep. This is all going away." He bent and kissed her brow. He didn't want her to see him go to the cabinet at the other end of the trailer and take out the 30.06. Quietly he chambered a single cartridge.

When he stepped out of the trailer, Joe Smith was standing not six feet away with the gun in his hand raised.

"Some partner," he said, and pulled the trigger, but the gun was silent. "What happened?" he asked. He looked closely at the gun. "Nothing in this goddamn world works." He looked up at Higgins.

"You didn't take off the safety," Higgins said, and shot him through the head.

Miranda sat stiffly in the wheelchair up against the porch railing of the small house. Higgins tucked a blanket in around her legs. Even here by the moderating sea, even at this distance from it, the night coming on was chill and damp in any onshore wind. The carob pods were filling quickly and lengthening. Back when they had first come here, the man who sold them the place, who had started the trees and raised them toward a market, told them how in a good season the pods might grow as much as an inch in one night. Higgins had tested that, had marked a hundred pods and measured them at dusk and again at dawn, and some had indeed grown an entire inch.

Now the smell of their growth mixed in the air with the ocean air.

"Good," Miranda said to him and smiled with half her mouth. The other half, the left, was hard and tight like the rest of her body on that side. "Good," she said again, and reached up her free hand to take his. He stood next to her, leaning against the railing. Together they looked out at the chip of ocean that they could see, watching it fade into darkness.

He imagined the sea voyage they and Joe Smith would have taken beyond the land, beyond the strictures of roads, the bonds of law, the plumb and the level of days. They would have gone outward to where there were only the endless parallels and meridians, merely imagined images of place, no more substantial than the lines that had run through Legion Street. Come, he would have taught Joe Smith. Jump.

Higgins watched the stars brighten in the darkness rushing on. He would rise to them. Miranda squeezed his hand. "Good," she said. "Good," holding him to earth. A freshening breeze swung the thousands and thousands of carob pods in a scurrying hiss, rising and falling like a wave washing over them, back and forth, washing over them, washing them away.

ILLINOIS SHORT FICTION

Crossings by Stephen Minot
A Season for Unnatural Causes by Philip F. O'Connor
Curving Road by John Stewart
Such Waltzing Was Not Easy by Gordon Weaver

Rolling All the Time by James Ballard
Love in the Winter by Daniel Curley
To Byzantium by Andrew Fetler
Small Moments by Nancy Huddleston Packer

One More River by Lester Goldberg
The Tennis Player by Kent Nelson
A Horse of Another Color by Carolyn Osborn
The Pleasures of Manhood by Robley Wilson, Jr.

The New World by Russell Banks
The Actes and Monuments by John William Corrington
Virginia Reels by William Hoffman
Up Where I Used to Live by Max Schott

The Return of Service by Jonathan Baumbach
On the Edge of the Desert by Gladys Swan
Surviving Adverse Seasons by Barry Targan
The Gasoline Wars by Jean Thompson

Desirable Aliens by John Bovey
Naming Things by H. E. Francis
Transports and Disgraces by Robert Henson
The Calling by Mary Gray Hughes

Into the Wind by Robert Henderson
Breaking and Entering by Peter Makuck
The Four Corners of the House by Abraham Rothberg
Ladies Who Knit for a Living by Anthony E. Stockanes